CHEAT
THE MOON

CHEAT
THE MOON

A NOVEL

PATRICIA HERMES

Little, Brown and Company
BOSTON NEW YORK TORONTO LONDON

First Edition

The characters and events portrayed in this book are fictitious.
Any similarity to real persons, living or dead, is coincidental and not
intended by the author.

Library of Congress Cataloging-in-Publication Data

Hermes, Patricia.
    Cheat the moon : a novel / Patricia Hermes. — 1st ed.
        p.   cm.
    Summary: With her mother dead and her father an alcoholic who
disappears for days at a time, Gabrielle must assume responsibility
for her younger brother, Will, and herself, barely making ends meet
and afraid to put her trust in anyone.
    ISBN 0-316-35929-7
    [1. Brothers and sisters — Fiction.   2. Fathers — Fiction.
3. Alcoholism — Fiction.   4. Poverty — Fiction.   5. Death — Fiction.]
I. Title.
PZ7.H4317Cf 1998
[Fic] — dc21   97–34369

10 9 8 7 6 5 4 3 2 1

MV-NY

Published simultaneously in Canada by Little, Brown & Company
(Canada) Limited

Printed in the United States of America

For Jennifer and her Paul

Chapter 1

"WILLIAM SHAKESPEARE BLAKELY!" I yelled. "Get in the house this minute!"

Will gave me his scared-rabbit look and scurried away from the rubbish heap, dropping a little bunch of sticks as he went. He snuffled, wiping the back of his hand across his nose. Up on the porch, he turned and looked at me, pleading almost, his thumb hovering near his mouth.

"You heard me!" I said. "This minute. And don't you go wiping your nose on your sleeve like that again. I have enough trouble getting your clothes clean as it is."

"But Gabby?" he pleaded. "Gabrielle?"

"Gabby, nothing!" I answered. "Get!"

Will looked away from me, his eyes fixed on the porch

floor, then hooked his thumb firmly inside his mouth. He turned away and disappeared into the house.

I waited till the screen door swung shut behind him, then turned back to clipping clothes onto the line.

I knew I had been mean to him — perhaps just a little harsh, Dad would say in his quiet way — and God knows I didn't want to be mean or harsh. But sometimes I got tired, too. And Will climbing around the rubbish heap, making men out of little sticks from the trash, armies of men and horses and cows and anything you could picture — well, it got to me sometimes, no telling why.

I finished clipping the clothes tight, watched the wind take a sheet and snap it around, take my favorite shirt, wrap it round and round like it was dancing with itself. The breeze was stiff enough to remind me that winter was still hanging about, but the sun was shining so bright it was hot almost. Sometimes we get wind roaring in across the land, cold enough to freeze us, and other times, like in spring and summer, there's no air at all and the heat sits right down here on top of us, not moving a bit. Mom used to say that's what Texas is all about — extremes of all kinds.

I looked down the path toward the road — a rocky kind of path leads from our house, all twisty and rutted, so we're sort of hidden-like from the main street. I wondered if it was worthwhile walking down to see if any mail had come. Not that I expected anything, really.

Still, one could never tell. Sometimes a person got lucky. I had been trying to be lucky, filling out every one of those contest things that kept coming, promising me a chance at a million dollars if I'd just return it with the right stickers attached before the deadline ran out. Once I got a different kind of contest, and I filled out a whole entire puzzle, answering questions about animals and furs and that sort of thing, and one day I got this letter, and they said I had won a fur coat. All I had to do was go to the store and fill out some papers, and it was mine.

That was one of the times I wished so hard for Mom, or a regular kind of dad, one who could tell me if this deal was on the up and up. But since Mom had died three years earlier, and since Dad was off somewhere again, God only knew where, there wasn't much chance of finding out about that fur coat. I had no intention of going into some store and finding out that they were just teasing me. A person could feel like a real fool that way.

Hard sometimes, with them both gone, although we managed. Sometimes it was easier about Mom, though — about her being dead, I mean, dead and in her grave, because at least that way, a person didn't keep on hoping. But Dad, he'd taken to drinking and going off and disappearing. He'd done that when Mom was alive, too, but nothing like the stretch that spring, when he'd sometimes be gone for a week or more. I still remember the look in Mom's eyes when he'd be gone even a day — that puzzled, disappointed look. I remember, too, how Dad would always promise it would never happen again. Still did promise that.

I looked up at the sky, at the sun moving so slow up there. I swear, some days I envy the sun, having nothing to do but get from east to west before the day is through. It stood almost straight over our heads — noontime — and I knew Will would be hungry by now.

Food. Food meant money.

It'd been more than a week since I'd seen Dad last, and the house money we kept in the coffee can was mostly gone. Course, I did have my secret supply — I'd opened my very own bank account with some Christmas money Clara sent — but that was for true emergencies. We were a long way from a true emergency, I knew that, seeing as how I had had a few of them already.

I started to turn and go back in the house then, thinking what I could make for Will and me to eat, when I heard a familiar sound: the old station wagon, its muffler gone, roaring and rattling onto the main street — Mr. Daniel Strong's car. Mr. Strong, he's near on a hundred years old, and sometimes I think his car is, too. I wonder why he doesn't get himself a new car, but I guess when you get that old, you don't want to start in on something new. Or maybe he just can't afford a new one.

I peered around the bend in our lane, looking to see

him drive up, wondered if he had anything new I might want to buy. Mr. Strong sells things from the back of his station wagon — well, from the back of his house, too, but that stuff, that you don't want anything to do with, whiskey or cigarettes.

What Mr. Strong sells from his station wagon, though, that's different. Sometimes he has stamps — those I could use, so I could send off my contest things. Maybe a new notebook. I'm always buying notebooks, can't get enough of them, I fill them up so fast. When I was little, I used to write stories in them, fairy tales or stories about smart girls who solved mysteries, but those mystery-solving girls, they mostly ended up sounding like pale little Nancy Drews, without any of the fun of the real Nancy. Lately, though, I'd been writing down other stuff, real things, about what it's like to be me, what I'm thinking and what's happening. I guess you could call it an autobiography, though who would want to read an autobiography of me, Gabrielle Thackeray Blakely from Marshall, Texas, Lord knows. Although Mom would have read it. Mom loved my writing — loved all kinds of writing and books, which is why, I guess, she gave me and Will the names she gave us.

I moved down the lane to the street and stood by the curb, watching Mr. Strong's big old yellow car come lumbering toward me. An old stray cat arrived from nowhere, began circling round and round my legs, like it had come to have a look, too.

Across the street, I saw Mallie's little brother, Les, come out on the porch, and then came Mallie, my best friend. School was out for the week, Easter week it was, so we were all free to be outside. Mallie had her arms folded over her chest, as if she was trying to hide it, not yet used to the way it had grown so sudden-like. I kind of knew how she felt, since mine was growing, too, but not big like hers. Mine were just little bumps, but they ached sometimes, and I could see they were going to grow soon, too.

Mallie lives in the fanciest house in town. She has two TVs and a big dish antenna so they can see all kinds of shows. They have two cars, one for her daddy and one for her mom, and nice clothes — really, really nice clothes, all of them from Kmart. Mallie even has a pink bedroom, with skirts on her bed and her dressing table, like something out of a magazine. And she and Les got mountain bikes as Easter presents — not even Christmas, just Easter! But Mallie is never show-offish about what she has, just plain. And she shares everything. Most times, though, I don't take from her, don't want to feel like I'm needy or anything. Although there are times I feel jealous, truth to tell, seeing that we have just this little box kind of house perched up on building blocks back up the lane, and not even one car. And even though we have a TV, you can only get but one channel on it. And clothes — Lord, that was a worry sometimes.

I waved to Mallie, then looked back up the lane to my

house and saw Will, still inside the screen door, looking out at me. Even from that far away, I could see the look on his face — hoping. I signaled to him.

"Come on!" I yelled to him. "You can come down now."

Dumb kid would stay put till the house burned down if I told him to.

He flew down the steps and down the path, looking both ways as he came — for dogs, I knew. He's terrified of dogs since he got bit when he was a baby practically. In seconds he was by my side, his hand slipping inside mine. His was all sweaty — snotty, too, I suspected — but I let him hold mine.

"What are you going to buy, Gabby?" he asked, his voice just a whisper. Will always speaks like that, can hardly ever get his voice above a whisper.

I shrugged. "Nothing. Just looking today," I said. "No money."

"Oh," Will said.

We waited till Mr. Strong had stopped his car and got out.

"Got real fine stuff today, Gabby," Mr. Strong said. "You just wait and see."

He went around his station wagon and opened up the back. He lifted out a big box and handed it out. I took it from him but handed it first to Will.

Will stood for a long minute, just looking down into the box, but he didn't even touch anything. He hardly ever bothers with Mr. Strong's stuff. For Will, his stick menagerie is all that seems to matter.

Will smiled up at me, then handed the box to me.

When I took it, I could see it was mostly junk in there — a bunch of buttons; a tiny metal car, its wheels missing; some jars filled with beads; a bottle of bubble stuff with a bubble wand, but it was half empty and the top was all rusted; a Barbie doll missing one arm. But no notebooks, no stamps.

I fingered the junk, pushed aside the buttons, and at the bottom of the box, saw something small — knobby and small.

I lifted it out, smiling a little. It was a doll, a doll no bigger than three inches long, made out of plastic, cracked from top to bottom like her two halves would split open and you'd have two dolls, a front and a back.

I had had a doll like that a long time ago — Evelyn, I'd named her — and she was even cracked the same way. I used to take her everywhere until I lost her. Lost her and cried for a week.

"It's Evelyn," Will whispered suddenly.

I looked down at him, frowning.

I'd lost Evelyn years ago, when Will was no more than about two. I remember clearly, because Mom was still here.

"Give it here," Mr. Strong said. "You don't want it, some other little girl will."

I dropped the doll back in the box and started to hand it to Mr. Strong.

But Will grabbed my arm. "Don't you want her?" he said.

I shook my head. "No money," I said.

"Wait!" Will said. He looked at Mr. Strong. "Wait!" he said again, his whispery voice straining to be heard. "I'll be back."

And he turned and ran from my side, back to the house.

"Ain't waiting long," Mr. Strong said, and he looked up the road then to Mallie's house. "Want to take a look-see?" he shouted.

Mallie just smiled, but she shook her head no, and Les, her brother, did, too.

I didn't blame them for not bothering. Mr. Strong mostly had junk.

I turned and watched Will. He had fled from my side, up the path to the house, his little feet flying, arms pumping. I saw him throw himself against the screen door, heard the door bang, and in just a minute, he was flying down the path again to where I stood.

"How much?" Will said breathlessly, his eyes fixed on Mr. Strong's face.

I grabbed Will's hand. "Don't be foolish!" I said. "We don't have money for foolishness."

Will shook off my hand. "How much?" he said again.

"Fifty cents," Mr. Strong said, holding out the little plastic doll. "Just five dimes."

"Here!" Will said.

He thrust something at Mr. Strong, but I stopped him, grabbing his wrist. "Give that to me," I said. "Where'd you get that?"

"They're mine!" Will said, pulling away from me again. "I saved up."

"You can't use it on this!" I said.

I squeezed his hand so hard, he cried out. A bunch of coins fell to the ground. Nickels and dimes and a bunch of pennies.

"Pick them up," I said.

Will looked at me, his little face pinched up tight.

I looked away from him, turned to Mr. Strong. "We don't want that doll thing." I said. "You can go."

Mr. Strong frowned, but he didn't say anything.

"You can go!" I said.

Will crouched down, then bent and scooped up the coins.

I saw how the back of his wrist was red, saw the marks from my fingers.

I bent to help him, gathered up the coins one by one, my fingernails scraping the dirt.

"Here," I said, and I handed the money back to him.

He didn't say anything, just closed his fist around the money.

We both stood up then, and together we turned and went up to the house.

"Gabby?" he said when we got to the porch.

"What?" I said.

"Nothing," he said.

"I hate it when you do that," I said, knowing I was being unfair. "I just hate it."

_Chapter 2 _

Uᴘ ɪɴ ᴛʜᴇ ʜᴏᴜsᴇ, I rummaged through the refrigerator and cabinets, looking to put together something for lunch.

Will had taken to building his stick people again, had them spread out all over the floor of the front room.

I took out some ham and beans and some cheese. I had cooked the ham and beans up good with salt pork, the way Dad likes them, done it over a week earlier, thinking maybe it'd keep Dad home for a time, but no, he was gone anyway, right after supper that night, actually. I should have known things like that by then, that no amount of good food or special treats — none of that would hold him here. Not even Will and me being extra good or extra quiet would make a difference. Sometimes I forgot, though. I felt as if a wind blew in and cleared out any brains I had, making me forget things I'd learned and should have held on to. But maybe that's how it is with a person's brains — they only remember half of what they're supposed to.

I cut the last bits of ham off the bone, put it together with the beans into a pot, and put the whole thing on the stove.

The entire time I was doing it, I was thinking how to find Dad again, whether to go into town looking. And then what to do if I couldn't find him. It had been eleven days now. True, I had my emergency supply of money in the bank, but I was scared to dip into that. And there was always Clara, always there in the back of my mind, although I'd never called on her — only met her that once, the time she came for Mom's funeral. She's Dad's grandmother, but she raised him up like he was her own child, seeing as how his mama died the minute he was born practically. But Dad didn't have anything to do with her, and I didn't know why. I only knew that when she came for Mom's funeral, Dad hardly spoke to her and couldn't wait for her to be gone. But she sent money sometimes, sent Will and me Christmas presents, sent Dad money once in a while during the year, too. So if I had to, I could go to her, but only if I really, really had to. No sense bringing in strangers who might mess things up even more than they were already messed.

But it wasn't only the money and food that worried

me — it was something even more. It was Will. Will had always been quiet, making no more sound than a baby bird, but when Dad was gone, Will got even quieter — paler, too, like all his energy went into wishing Dad back. I wanted to shake him sometimes, tell him no one could make Dad come back, no one but Dad himself. He'd come back when he was good and ready, on his own time.

But what if he was gone for a whole month, like he was that winter when Will got sick? I couldn't help thinking sometimes that missing Dad was what had made Will sick, worrying and missing him so hard. I guess maybe, with Mom having died and left us, that's why it was especially hard on Will when Dad went off. Me, I'm older, so it wasn't so hard. And I understood more.

I went to the window, looked out across the field in back. Sometimes Dad would come that way, avoiding the road, keeping back out of sight of neighbors since there's not another house behind us — just fields back there, and the hills that begin climbing slowly up to the mountain. Dad seemed to think no one knew about his off times, the times he'd just disappear off the face of the earth. But they knew, like that Ms. McIntosh at school, always asking questions.

A mockingbird was swooping, dipping and calling, the sweetest kind of summer song, yet it was a long ways till summer, just past Easter now.

Stupid old mockingbird, not even knowing what was what. I sighed.

A lot like you sometimes, the voice said inside my head.

Hush up! I muttered silently.

It was the voice again, my voice. I heard it sometimes, right inside my head, and it was as clear as if someone was talking to me. When it had first started happening, I thought it was Mom, because it started right after she died, but then I realized that it didn't say the kinds of things she would have said. My voice mocked me, made fun of me — well, not always making fun, but always pointing out the bad side of things. And it was clear all right, a real voice, so I knew it was a real person, and I even knew it was a girl person, even if I didn't know who she was or what she was doing walking around inside my head.

Used to be, I had been scared of the voice, scared that hearing it meant I was crazy. So I hadn't told anybody, not even Mallie. I was afraid she'd think I was totally weird, maybe even crazy, even though I knew she wouldn't tell anyone even if she did think so. But when I did tell her one day, she didn't think it was weird or crazy at all. In fact, she said, she thought it was kind of sweet. She said lots of people talk to people who aren't there, like talking to the angels and to God and stuff, and sometimes, she said, they even got answers to their talking, their prayers. And nobody thinks that's crazy. So I felt a whole lot better after that.

Anyway, sometimes the voice spoke up and sometimes it shushed up. But always, I knew it was there, a part of me.

Across the field, the wind suddenly gusted through the grass, rippling it, waving it. Mom always said that that's how the ocean looked — her ocean, up in Maine, where she came from. It went in waves, just like the fields, she said, ripples and swelling movements of wind and tides.

Mom missed the ocean. You could see it in her eyes when she talked about it, that lonesome look she got. And she promised me that someday I'd see it with her.

But she broke that promise.

Funny how promises are. I remember Dad promising Mom he'd never again leave us. After each of his off times he promised the same thing — never, he said. And I remember when Mom was sick, how he promised her anything, the world, he said, if she'd get better. And she tried to get better; I know she did. The doctor tried, too, but I guess that disease thing had been working away at her insides for a long time before they found it, and by then it was too late. And then, after Mom died, Dad, well, he seemed to forget his promise.

Across the field, the wind died down, and then there was another smaller ripple of grass, in just one place, like something small was moving along in there — an armadillo maybe, maybe even some sort of a snake.

I shuddered. I hate snakes.

I smelled the beans cooking, turned back to the stove, and stirred them.

I looked through the doorway to where Will was playing quiet-like on the floor, always quiet.

Once, long ago, just to stir him up, see if there was any kind of spark to him, I tiptoed up right behind him where he was playing, and I shouted, right in his ear.

But he didn't even yell, didn't even get mad at me. He just looked at me, that wide-eyed lonesome look, and then I felt like a bit of trash, and I never did it again. Not even once.

But Lord, how I wished to see some spark, some sound at least out of him. Because I was scared, scared that he was becoming more like a rabbit every day, and we had to hold on, hold on and stand up for ourselves. And if Dad didn't come back, we'd have to take care of ourselves. Just him and me. And him just a little kid. But if you have to be a kid on your own, you better be a tough little kid. And the sooner he found that out, the better.

I stood in the doorway, watching him, his head bent, that gash from the dog bite still showing white and ragged, like a zipper mark on the back of his neck.

He had an entire army of people made now, from tiny little ladies to big tall men to itty-bitty babies. He's practically a genius with this kind of thing, and I think he could be a real fine artist. It's truly amazing to see the way he takes some sticks, ties them with a bit of string or wire or whatever he has around — and a creature appears. I watched him now, making a horse for himself.

"Gabby?" he said.

He hadn't looked up, and I knew I hadn't made a sound. How had he known I was there?

"What?" I said, and my voice came out harsher than I meant it to.

"I'm thinking something," he said.

"Yeah?" I said.

"About Daddy," he whispered.

So what could I say about that? Nothing. "You hungry?" I asked.

He nodded.

"Good," I said. "Me, too. Beans are cooking."

He was quiet a minute, and then he said, "Gabby?"

"What now?" I said.

"Is there enough? Food, I mean? And money?"

"There's enough," I said. "Don't you go worrying your head. We'll make out all right. Food and money are my worry, not yours. Now, go wash your hands."

I went back to the kitchen, dished the ham and beans out onto two plates, and poured some water into glasses for each of us.

Will had gone to wash up, and while I waited, I went to stand by the window again.

The tall grasses and weeds in the fields were still now; the mockingbird, too, had stilled. Only a red-winged blackbird clung to the side of a reed, swaying with the wind.

Funny how bleak those red-winged blackbirds look, till they spread their wings, showing their brilliant red and yellow stripes. I remembered how Mom had told me once that red-winged blackbirds are a lot like little girls — ordinary enough to look at, till they spread their wings and fly. And when I told her little girls couldn't fly, Mom just looked at me and said, "Says who?"

But Mom always thought nonsense kinds of thoughts, things that made no sense to most people — like the business about the moon. When I was little, I was scared on nights of the full moon, I think because I saw a show once that said that werewolves and bad things come out on full-moon nights. When I told Mom that, she looked real hard at me, and then she took me by the shoulders and she looked right into my eyes. "Cheat the moon, Gabrielle," she said. "Cheat the moon."

And when I asked how to do that, she just laughed. "You'll figure it out," she told me, hugging me close. "You will. You'll figure it out."

I sighed. Nonsense, it was nonsense, but I missed her still. Missed her like anything. I think I especially missed her nonsense talk.

I turned back to the table and looked at what was on the plates.

Well, we had enough food, and when it was used up, there was always peanut butter. Anyway, maybe by supper, Dad would be back.

"Come on, Will," I called. "Let's eat."

He came quietly into the kitchen, sliding into his chair with no more fuss than if he were a shadow.

He looked down at his plate, then closed his eyes for a minute.

I knew what he was doing — praying. Dumb little kid. Like God was going to come down here Himself and bless this food.

I just shook my head and picked up my fork. Didn't matter. Let him believe if it made him happier.

Chapter 3

W HEN THE DAY WAS DONE and I'd helped Will get washed up and into bed, and I'd talked to him and read to him the way I do most every night, I went out on the porch to sit awhile, taking my notebook with me. I had so many things to write about. This time of year, spring, well it seemed to pull and push at me, demanding that I write down everything — like how even the skunk cabbages seemed to come alive in the moonlight, all green and sprouty all of a sudden, their spikes reaching for the sky, about how the moon seems to rise up so sudden-like, you'd think a great hand was pushing it right over the hills there. Down back of the house by the marsh, I could hear the spring frogs starting up, a whole chorus of them, one yelling its brains out to the other, and I wanted to write them down, too. But there was so much, that instead of writing, I just did nothing but look. And listen.

I swear, each spring it's like a whole frog chorus has come to town, each determined to outshout the other. Peepers, they're called, spring peepers, but how can you say this kind of racket is made by something peeping? Peeping I always thought was like a whisper, the kind of sound a mother bird makes maybe, the kind of sound Mom used to make, when she'd whisper to Will when he was a baby, whisper and sing to him. I wrote that down a long time ago, about how Mom reminded me of a mother bird, and Will a bothersome baby bird, mouth open, always his mouth open, to nurse, to yell.

I looked up at the moon now, wondered if Mom knew about us, worried about us. Did she know where Dad was?

I sighed, knowing I had to go into town, looking for him. I had decided that at lunchtime, looking at Will, so quiet there in his chair, eating like a little bird again, but not a hungry, yelling bird, just an automatic, fake kind of bird, opening his mouth and taking in food, over and over, not saying a word. I had to get Dad home for him.

It would be hard — I'd done it enough times before to know — Dad leaning heavy on my arm, stumbling, then stopping to vomit all over, sometimes right on his shoes, sometimes on mine, and then I'd have to stop and clean us both up. But he'd be home, off the streets with us, where it was safe, no drink. Then he could rest and get better, and I knew he'd be good enough for a while, maybe long enough to work a few weeks and bring in some money. Even though I knew he'd be gone again soon enough. Come and go. Come and go.

A good man, that's what Mom always said about Dad. He was a good man.

Was he? I don't know. When he was good — sober — he usually managed to find some work, and that kept us in food for a while. Food and some clothes, and enough school supplies that we didn't feel ashamed to go to school, always having to borrow a paper or a pencil off of somebody.

Funny, when Dad was gone, I didn't think about him much, except to worry about where we'd get food or about Will and such. But I dreamed about him. Every single night, I dreamed the same dream: I was in this big old house, trying to fix it up, trying to make it pretty. I was putting pictures and things on the walls, covering up holes, but no matter what I did, I couldn't make it quite right. And then I'd look up and there he was, standing in the doorway, watching me. I'd start to tell him about what I was doing, but he'd point to the wall behind me, and I'd turn and there'd be a big hole in the wall, and people looking in.

Strange. Strange to believe that I even bothered to dream about him. But I needed to go find him for Will.

Will and Dad, they'd always been a pair. You'd never find one without the other when Dad was home. They had these little games they'd play with the stick men and twigs. And Dad was always telling Will stories, and he put Will in the stories, and in the stories, Will was always fine and brave. I wondered sometimes if maybe Dad knew, too, how important it was for Will to stop being a scared rabbit, to be a tough kid.

I watched the moon rise higher over the hill and thought about going to town. I hated going there, hated sticking my head into those bars, hated the way people looked at me. I could tell they felt sorry for me. But I could tell they thought other things, too. And men, they thought things I didn't want to think about at all.

I stood up then, went to the edge of the porch and stood looking over the night and the fields. The wind had died, and there was no whisper of that kind of wind that moved the grass in waves like it had earlier. It was just a regular, quiet Texas night, the moon shining strong on everything, making it so bright that I knew I could sit and read my whole notebook, sit myself down and read it all the way through if I wanted to.

For a long time I stood there, thinking about that, thinking about maybe sitting awhile, resting, reading. I could wait one more day before looking for Dad, couldn't I?

But then I told myself, *Do it now. Get it over with.* Besides, it was the perfect night for walking to town. With the moonlight, I'd have no trouble finding my way, no fear of stepping on snakes or surprising a polecat on its prowls. Too bright for ghosts, too — haunts, Dad always called them. Not that I believe in ghosts. But sometimes at night, I'd noticed, sometimes your brain plays tricks on you, makes you believe things that you wouldn't believe in the bright light of daytime. Like when I used to believe in werewolves.

I turned, took my notebook back into the house, and slid it in my hiding place under my mattress. Then I tiptoed to Will's room.

I stood over his bed, watching him sleep.

His thumb was in his mouth, and every little while, he'd suck hard, making little slurpy sounds. Then he'd stop, breathe easy, and his thumb would slide out of his mouth. And then, with a jerk, he'd push it back in. The other hand he kept curled around the back of his neck, like he was protecting that scar place.

I worried about that thumb sucking a little. At six years old, wasn't he kind of old to be sucking his thumb? Sometimes on the playground at school, I'd look around at the other kindergarten kids, to see if any of them sucked their thumbs. But they didn't. Maybe, though, they did it in secret, like at night when they were in bed, just like Will.

Suddenly Will began to breathe more rapidly, panting a little, like he was running. And he made little sounds, whimpering sounds, like he was being chased.

I bent and tugged the cover up under his chin.

"Hush," I whispered. "You just hush now."

As if he had heard me in his sleep, the whimpering stopped and he began slurping on his thumb again.

I turned then and tiptoed out of the room.

"Gabby?" he said.

I spun around.

"What are you doing awake?" I said.

"Are you going to town?" Will whispered.

"What business is it of yours?" I said.

"I just asked," he said.

I came back and sat myself on the edge of his bed.

He sat up and looked at me, the old shirt of Dad's he wore to bed twisted up around him, his hair all mussed up and curling around his ears.

I hate the way his hair curls, am always trying to clip it or wet it and comb it down. Curled like that, it makes him look too much like a — I don't know — a baby or something.

I sighed and looked out the window. "I guess, Will," I said. "I guess so." I looked down at him. "You'll be all right here if I go?"

He nodded. "Will you find him?" he whispered. "Will he come home with you?"

I shrugged.

He looked up at me, then away. His thumb drifted toward his mouth.

I grabbed his hand and held it tight. "Will," I said. "Listen — the frogs are calling. Know what that means?"

He just looked at me.

"It means spring is coming," I said. "And when spring comes, then summer comes. And you know what that means?"

Even in the dark, I could see Will smile. "No school," he said.

"And what else?" I said.

It was a game Will and I played, one I'd made up one time when Dad had been gone a long time and all Will could think about and talk about was Dad. I made up a game to make him think about what was good — what was good that was going to happen. Even without Dad at home.

"What else?" I said now, prompting him. "What else happens in summer? You know."

"Blackberries," he said.

"Right," I said. "And?"

"And fireflies!" he said.

"And?" I said.

"Swimming in the creek," he said.

"And?" I said.

He didn't answer.

"Come on," I said. "What else?"

He sighed. "I don't want to play that game anymore," he said.

"Yes, you do," I said. "You do, too. How about frogs, and sleeping on the porch, and no shoes, and . . ."

He sighed again. "And sun that's hot. And stories — you tell me stories in summer."

"Right," I said.

I ran a hand over his head, smoothed down his hair.

"G-G-Gabby?" he said.

"What?" I said.

"Say you'll find him," he whispered. "Say it."

"I can't, Will!" I said. "I don't know."

I pushed him gently back on his pillow and pulled the covers up to his chin. "Now, you sleep," I said. "Nothing's going to hurt you while I'm gone. You listen to the frogs, okay? And sleep. Promise?"

He didn't answer.

"Come on, promise!" I said.

"You promise," he whispered.

"Me?" I said.

"Say you'll find him," he said.

"How can I promise that?" I said. "I said I'd look, okay?"

"But what if . . ." He grabbed at my hand, held it tight. "You know."

"No, I don't know," I said, mad-like.

He didn't say anything, just held my hand tight awhile.

I pulled away from him.

"You're being a baby," I said.

He was quiet.

"A big old baby!" I said. I stood up. "Now, I'll be back in a while. You stay right here in this bed, you hear? I don't want to have to worry about you, too, see?"

He didn't answer. But in the light from the moon, I could see him nod.

"Promise?" I said.

Again I saw him nod. I saw, too, how his thumb drifted back to his mouth.

_ Chapter 4 _

THAT WALK TO TOWN was fair enough, what with the moon shining and the mockingbirds calling in the dark, the way they do only in spring and early summer, and the sound of the wind sighing all about. It made it seem almost peaceful, like I was just out for a stroll to town.

But when I got to town, the peaceful part was over. I dreaded looking in bars, feeling people's eyes on me, knowing they were half sorry for me, half laughing at me.

I stood outside Wanda's Bar, the first on the street, and went over in my head the things that helped: *Breathe easy. Stand up tall. Look men square in the eye like you're not scared of them or anything. And if Dad's there, just take his arm, lead him out gently* — he would usually come right with me, as long as I kept talking to him. *So tell him about Will, remind him about how he and Will can do things together in the morning.* Although it usually took a lot more than just one morning for Dad to be able to even get out of bed.

I took a deep breath, stood straight as I could get, and put my shoulders back. Then I marched into Wanda's.

When I looked around, I could tell Dad wasn't there, didn't even have to ask, the place practically empty. But Wanda, she saw me, said she'd not seen him in a while.

I left fast, then went on to Marsha and Tom's, the next one down the block. That place was almost empty, too, just three men sitting at the bar, and Tom behind the bar, nobody talking, all of them doing nothing but holding on to a glass of something and staring up at a TV. It was the same there: no Dad. Nobody had seen him.

Tom, though, he gave me this look, like he was thinking something or knew something. But when I said, "What?" he just shook his head and said, "He'll turn up. Always does."

The last place, the place that was always awful, was Dally's. It was the last one on the street, and Dad's favorite. Looked like everybody's favorite, from the men I could see through the window, from the sound and light spilling out onto the street.

I stopped outside awhile, getting up my courage. Empty bars were bad enough. Crowded bars, they were something else.

Well, nothing to do but go in.

Bet he's not there! my voice said.

Maybe, I thought. *But I have to look.*

And I did — pushed open the door and went inside. It was real noisy in there, men and women clumped at the bar, more men in back, hooting and squabbling over a dart game, the TV over the bar blaring some sport or other, baseball, I think.

Nobody seemed to notice me, or if they did, they didn't care that I was there. I made my way through the crowd, looking at the backs of people at the bar, knowing I'd recognize Dad even from behind. Then, when I didn't see him anywhere, I began poking into booths, staring into faces that looked back at me, surprised or curious or sometimes mad-like at being snooped on.

I had just reached the back, the dart game, when someone spoke to me.

"Hey, Gal!" the voice said.

I turned and saw Joseph smiling down at me.

"What are you doing here?" he asked. And then he added softly, "Your pa?"

I nodded.

"Haven't seen him," Joseph said. "Not for a while."

"When?" I said. "Do you remember?"

He pulled his eyebrows together, shook his head. "Not since about . . ." He shook his head again. "Give me a minute," he said. "Francie might know."

He turned, and I watched him make his way toward the front, watched his huge head and shoulders towering over everyone else in the room.

I followed him, pushing my way through the crowd. I've always liked Joseph. He's been a friend since I was a tiny little girl, maybe because he was a friend of Mom's. He's the biggest person I've ever seen. His hair is dark and straight and very long, and he wears it tied in a kind of ponytail that lies flat against his back. His arms are big and muscled — he told me once it was from working in the oil fields a long time ago. He has a shop in town with a sign that says *Shoemaker*, but it's really an everything shop. He mends harnesses, puts new soles on people's shoes, does anything they need. He even does a little doctoring stuff, telling people which herbs to use for hurt backs and which will help colicky babies. But his wife, Francie, she's the real expert on herbs, grows them and even goes out and gathers stuff from the woods and fields. Sometimes after school or on summer days, I come and sit in Joseph's shop and watch him. He lets me sit, and even though he hardly ever speaks, we're always really comfortable together. He told me once, "If there's nothing worth saying, then don't say anything."

I followed him now, wondering about Francie, if she'd seen Dad, if she'd remember when she'd last seen him. It was really dark in there, noisy, too, but the worst part was the smell. I always forget how bad a bar smells, closed up like that, settled in on itself.

I tried not to breathe too deep, inched toward the door, following Joseph, looking for Francie.

Then, just as I got near the door, an arm reached out from the bar and circled my waist, hard and rough.

"Hey, girl," a voice said. "What are you doing here? Looking for me?"

It was Dad's friend, sort of friend, I guess, Harry. I'd met him in there before, other times I'd had to come. He held me so tight, I could barely breathe.

"My dad," I said. "You've seen him?"

"Now what do you want with your old pa when you got me?" Harry answered.

He pulled me closer, lifting me so I was half on his lap, his mean old breath almost suffocating me. I leaned my face away from him, as far away as I could.

"Let go," I said.

He just breathed at me, his wet eyes running up and down all over me. He made me want to do just what my friend Mallie does — fold my arms tight over my chest, don't let him see nothing.

But I couldn't move my arms at all, the way he had one trapped at my side, the other pressed between his side and mine.

"No hurry," he said. "No hurry. You just stay right here on my lap, sweet as can be."

"Let go!" I said again. And I twisted real hard to get away. And still, I couldn't move.

He leaned closer then, his whiskery chin gray and pockmarked, so close that his beery breath, stale and vinegary, was practically choking me. I wriggled and turned, and when I did, I saw some men at the bar watching — watching and laughing.

Again I twisted, but again I was crushed up close, so close I could feel his ribs through his shirt.

"Please !" I said. "Please let go."

I was just fixing to kick him, had pulled back my foot, when suddenly a hand appeared, an enormous hand.

It came between my face and Harry's, forcing his head back away from me. Then, quick as anything, another hand clamped down on the top of Harry's head. It forced his head down toward the bar, hard to the bar.

Both Harry's hands flew up, and suddenly I heard a crunching sound, heard his teeth click hard together as his chin slammed into the bar.

He had let go of me when the hands grabbed him — Joseph's hands — and I went staggering toward the floor. But Joseph caught me up, set me on my feet, real gentle-like.

"Come on, Gal," he said. "Let's go outside."

He took my arm, led me out of that place.

We stood on the sidewalk, both of us breathing hard — I was practically gasping — but when Joseph spoke, he sounded calm, like nothing had happened at all.

"Francie hasn't seen your daddy," he said quietly. "Not for more than a week now. But I'll be on the lookout for him. I'll bring him home, Gal. Don't you worry. Get on home now."

"I'm going," I said, and I left.

I hurried down the street, willing my mind to settle down, taking deep breaths, pushing away the picture of Harry's whiskered face in front of mine, trying to see instead Joseph's dark eyes, hear his quiet voice. Then, just as I got to the end of the street, just before I got to the path that led through the field, I realized I'd forgotten to say thank you.

I turned then and saw Joseph still watching me. I lifted a hand, and he lifted his back, and then he turned and went back into the bar.

I walked on home, my heart hammering, my mind in a tizzy fit, all the restfulness of the spring night seeming to be gone. Even the mockingbirds had stopped their singing, and the peepers weren't yelling. The moon, too, was clouded over, streaks and wisps of clouds floating across, blocking its light, like a storm was brewing somewhere close.

Stupid Harry.

Stupid Dad.

Stupid world.

By the time I got home, my heart had finally stopped hammering wildly and my breathing was almost normal.

I climbed the porch steps and went inside, knowing I had to tell Will: no Dad. When I looked in on him, he was, like I'd figured, wide awake.

He was sitting straight up in bed, but as soon as he saw me, his thumb drifted right into his mouth. He didn't even ask, knew by looking that there was no Dad, maybe by hearing my footsteps outside before he even saw me — just one set of footsteps.

"I'm sorry," I said. And I shook my head at him. "I'm sorry, Will.

His thumb was firmly in his mouth then, and he lay down and turned his face to the wall.

Chapter 5

Next week was back to school, Easter vacation over, and on that Monday, like always before school, I scrubbed Will so hard he was shining. He was pretty red, too, where I used that washrag so hard, rubbing behind his ears and around his neck, although I was careful, as usual, around that old scar. I always scrubbed him up like that, made sure we both were clean and decent. Most of our clothes were kind of shabby-like — Will's pants were thin, and I had just one skirt and one pair of jeans, and the jeans were getting short. I'd thought of adding on a bit at the bottom of them, like I'd seen someone do on a TV sewing show. But I'd have to get some material from somewhere to do that with. Anyway, we were clean. You had to say that for us.

When we were both scrubbed and ready, we set off for

school. We waited down the street, at the foot of Mallie's driveway, for Mallie and her brother, Les, to come on and join us.

Mostly I like going to school, but sometimes it's hard, hard because the teachers ask questions — like, "How's things at home?" *Like, it's none of your business,* I want to tell them, but of course I don't. I just smile and say, "Fine, thank you." For a while, it got really, really bad because there's this social worker, Ms. McIntosh, who comes to our school on Mondays twice a month. She began taking me and Will both out of class — but not together, one at a time. I told Will not to tell her anything, and that wasn't hard for Will. He told me that they just played blocks together, didn't even talk.

But me, Ms. McIntosh would ask me things like, "Is your dad at home?" and "How are you making out?" and "Do you need anything?" I put up with that for four different Mondays, and then one day I told her it was downright rude to ask such personal things, and how would she like it if I asked her how things were in her house and where her daddy was? She just looked at me and wrote down everything I said, and I told her that was rude, too. Next time she came to get me out of class, I wouldn't even look at her, and I just shook my head no.

So she's finally stopped bothering me, and instead she takes Missy Dejunes from class. Missy's kind of slow and sometimes goes for days and days wearing the same faded yellow T-shirt, even sleeping in it, it looks like. So I guess she and Ms. McIntosh have something to talk about.

While Will and I waited for Mallie and Les, Will bent to the dirt and picked up some twigs. He looked at each one real close, throwing some away, choosing others to put in his pocket. It seemed like he already knew which ones would go where in one of his stick men or children or animals.

He didn't speak, hadn't said but about two words since I'd come back that night without Dad, and I was getting mighty bothered by him. But I knew enough by then to just let him be. Sooner or later, he'd start to talk, at least once Dad got back. No sense forcing him.

When Mallie and Les came out, Mallie quick ran down the drive to where I waited. She grabbed my arm, holding me some steps back behind Les and Will as they started off together.

"Guess what?" she said, all excited-like.

"I don't know," I said. "What?"

"Guess!" she said. She did this little dance, jiggling from one foot to the other, then twirling around, her wiry gold hair flying out and away from her head.

I had to smile at her. With Mallie, everything is always extra excited-like. The way she walks, even the way she talks is fancy — choosing the fanciest words, things you only read in books but hardly ever hear real people say.

Her mama says she acts like she's on fire half the time, and I think that's about right. She reminds me of an electric wire I saw one time that came down in a summer storm. It lay on the ground, showering out sparks and making crackling sounds, wriggling around with this wild life of its own.

"Come on, guess," she said again, twirling close to me. "It's a delicious surprise."

"You won a million dollars," I said.

"Stop it!" she said.

"You're getting a new dress," I said.

"Nope."

"New shoes?"

"Nope."

"Your dad's getting a new car."

She sighed. "Oh, I wish!" she said. "But he's not."

"New pet?" I said. "A horse?"

"Better even," she said.

"I don't know!" I said.

"Then I'll tell you," Mallie said. She turned and smiled me. "We're going away this summer! A vacation. A glamorous vacation."

She was watching me, eyes wide, waiting for my reaction.

"But you always go on vacation in summer," I said. "To your nana —"

"Uh-uh," she said. "Not this time. Guess where we're going this time."

I rolled my eyes. "To Alaska," I said, a little tired of her guessing game.

"Silly!" She made a face, then grabbed my arm, pulling me close to her. "We're going to the ocean, that's what! The Atlantic Ocean! Where there are waves and where we can swim and maybe see dolphins and sharks. And on the way, we're going to stop in New York City and see skyscrapers and subways and everything."

"Wow," I said, pulling back and looking at her. "You are lucky. Really, really lucky."

And I meant it. Not because of New York. But the ocean. How I've wanted to see the ocean. Mallie knew that, knew because we were always talking about it. But she dreamed of New York, was going to be a dancer there someday.

I dreamed of the ocean. Of dolphins. Of gulls. Of blue-gray waves.

"I *am* lucky," Mallie said. She got this secret, sly look on her face, and she began smiling at me. "But you are, too."

She ran ahead a few steps, spun around, then turned and started walking backwards, facing me.

We had already walked down the main street and had come to the edge of town where we take the shortcut through the field.

Up beyond Mallie, I could see Will and Les start off into the field, walking side by side, Will's little head now almost hidden by the tall weeds.

"So guess again," Mallie said.

"You're going on a plane," I said, "and you're going to stay in hotels, and eat out at restaurants on fancy plates with tablecloths and real flowers and —"

"You're being silly," she said. "But okay, if you won't guess, I'll tell you."

She danced back to my side and took my arm again. "You're coming with us!" she said, laughing. And then she repeated it, real slowly. "You. Are. Coming. With. Us!"

I pulled away and frowned at her. "Uh-uh," I said. "Am not."

"Are too," she said. "Cross my heart." She made an X sign on her chest.

"Me?" I said. "How come?"

Mallie laughed and danced away again, her arms thrown out in an exaggeration of a dancer's pose. Then she turned, walking backwards again and smiling at me. "Because my mother said so. We're going in a camper and she said we have room for an extra person because the camper is so big. And Mom said it could be you. She even suggested it be you."

I took a deep breath. A vacation. I'd never been on a vacation. And I've never, ever been to the ocean.

"Maine?" I said.

"Main what?" Mallie said.

"The state of Maine?" I asked. "Is that where you're going to the ocean?"

Mallie shrugged. "All over. We're camping. New York, like I told you. Rhode Island. Maine if we get there."

I took a deep breath and looked out over the field. Maine. The gray waves breaking on the rocks, the way Mom used to tell me. The ocean looking like fields of grain — blue fields of grain, gray fields, Mom said. "The sound, not like anything you've ever heard, Gabrielle. It rushes, and soothes, and sometimes it seems to whisper to you. And the moon rests on the water, and it looks like two moons sometimes, Gabrielle, twin moons, and . . ."

And . . . I couldn't go.

I looked at Mallie, felt tears come to my eyes, and I quick looked away.

"You're crying!" Mallie said. "You silly thing! You're crying. But I know, I almost cried, too, when Mom told me. I know."

I just shook my head. She didn't know. And I couldn't tell her.

Because there was no possible way I could go. No possible way I could leave Will.

Unless . . . oh, if only Dad would come back! Only once was he gone for longer than this, that time he was gone for a month.

But even then, even then I couldn't go, couldn't trust him with Will.

But Mom had said he was a good man — she'd said so.

A good man? my voice spoke up. *Ha. Like you could trust*

him? What if he walks out and leaves Will alone when you're gone?

"You're going to love it," Mallie said, walking quietly beside me now, some of the electric feeling seeming to have quieted inside her. "Two whole weeks," she said dreamily. "You and me, and we'll see the whole country practically, maybe see places we'll live in someday. Maybe I can see some places in New York where I'll dance. And you can see the ocean, where you'll write. And when we come back home, we can picture where we'll live. Then when we're grown up, you can visit me in the city and I'll show you all the delicious restaurants, and I'll come for vacations at the ocean and you can show me your dolphins that you've trained, and the books you've written with all the dolphin pictures . . . and doesn't that sound exquisite?"

I took a deep breath. It did sound . . . exquisite. The whole thing.

But I shook my head.

I couldn't go. I just couldn't.

But I wished so much. And in spite of myself, I even began to dream.

__Chapter 6__

FOR THAT WHOLE NEXT WEEK, that's all Mallie talked about — the vacation, the camping. The ocean.

She kept pestering me to promise her I would go, but I kept putting her off. Mallie and me, we have no secrets from each other, so she knew full well about Dad, that he was away, that this was one of his off times again. But she kept saying, "He'll come back soon. He can care for Will, and anyway, it's not till June that we go." But it was already almost the beginning of May, with no sign of him. Twenty whole days he'd been gone. If he were anywhere around, Joseph would have brought him home. So how could I promise? And besides, even if he did come home — could I trust him to stay there with Will till I came back?

One thing for sure! — I didn't tell Will about the trip.

Knowing him, he'd want me to go, and it would be just one more worry for him.

Anyway, vacation aside, I had other worries. I had begun dipping into our emergency supply of money, taken twenty dollars out of the bank on Saturday. I had shopped careful-like, bought just the things we absolutely needed, like bread and milk and laundry detergent, and also a treat for Will, those Devil Dogs he loves. I knew if I kept being wise, we could get by for another week on what I'd bought, maybe longer even.

I knew, too, that summer was coming on. School would be over. There's always farm work, picking to do, and we'd manage. Like always. And of course, if things got really bad — like if he never came back — there was Clara. I hated thinking about that, though, calling on someone I didn't even know. What if she was like that Ms. McIntosh, that bossy social worker, sticking her nose into our business? But I couldn't see me just asking Clara for money and telling her to leave us alone.

And then I thought about Will and how silent he'd become. He hadn't said a word in days practically.

I rehearsed in my head what I would say if I called Clara: "Hello, Nana. It's me, Gabrielle."

No, *Nana* sounded too cozy for somebody I'd met just once.

Then maybe: "Hello, Clara. It's me, Gabby. Could I come and stay with you awhile, Will and me, both? . . . No, nothing's wrong. I'd just like to see you again."

I shook my head at myself. Why would she want to see us now when she'd only ever seen us once in her whole life?

Anyway, even if she turned out to be a nice enough lady, she surely wasn't a moron. She'd know what was what.

Still, I knew where she lived if I needed her, and I even had the exact address — the town and even the street and number — had it from the letters she sent to Dad four, five times a year. She sent money in the letters, too. I knew that because once I opened a letter, since Dad had been gone a long time, and why not? I used the money, too, for food, but never told Dad about it.

Dad, whenever I asked about her, he always frowned and his eyes got that hard, flat look, and he said not to worry my head. I had an idea about it, my own feeling from something Mom said once. Mom said Dad shouldn't be ashamed — shouldn't be, she said, because it was all long ago and he was just a child then. But when I asked her what it was he was ashamed of but shouldn't be, she just shook her head. And that was the last time she'd mentioned it.

Anyway, I thought about all these things, as day followed day with no Dad, night followed night. And me still thinking of that ocean. Back and forth I went in my head, my thoughts like a Ping-Pong ball, thinking one minute he'd show up, thinking the next that this time he was gone for good. Back and forth, back and forth. One night was especially bad for the Ping-Pong ball thoughts, so I gave up trying for sleep, got up, and went to the porch to sit, taking my notebook with me.

It was warming up fast, but not yet summer, and I took a quilt with me, wrapped it around myself.

I pulled up my feet, tucked them inside the quilt, looked up at the stars and the moon full overhead. I opened my notebook and began to write — write about what I heard:

> *A bird sings — a mockingbird, the only bird I know that sings in the night. By midnight or so, it will stop: you hardly ever hear a mockingbird after midnight. I wonder a lot about what makes a mockingbird sing when all God's other creatures are asleep.*
>
> *Well, that's not exactly true that all creatures are asleep. Night things — nocturnal things, Mom used to call them — are out and about, and when I was little, I was scared of those odd and fearsome things, like bats and owls and mice and stuff — and the were-wolves that I imagined. Only one good thing about full moon nights, I used to think: at least on full moons, you get to see what's what.*

I put the pencil and notebook down, leaned back in the chair, and looked up at the night sky and the moon. I remembered one night, one full-moon night, I think I was just about six, and Will, he was just a baby. I remember Mom came outside with me and took me in her lap and we sat right here on this very porch, looking up at the moon. I can still remember the song Mom sang about the moon — she made it up, I know, because I never heard it anywhere else, and besides, she always put me in her songs, just like Dad puts Will in his stories. So that night, she was singing about the stars, and how they sing songs to the moon, and how the moon talks back. And just as she was singing, a coyote appeared, came right up to the steps, stood right there, and looked at us, its silver eyes shining in the moonlight.

I pressed closer in Mom's arms, but Mom, she just laughed and rocked me, and she looked back into the coyote's silver eyes. In a while, that coyote turned and hightailed it back out on the plains, its body slung low to the ground. For a long time after, I wouldn't go out on the porch at night again, not even with Mom. I figured it was the moon itself that had brought the coyote out to stare at me, just like it drew out the bats and owls and mice. And the werewolves. And Mom, she told me again: "Cheat the moon, Gabrielle. Cheat it out of its fearsome things. Make it bring only the good things." But she died without ever telling me how to make it work that way.

I sighed, pulled the quilt tighter around my shoulders, looked around. Above me, the moon lit the fields and the trees, making the gray weathered porch and railings all silvery. The house hadn't been painted since — when? Probably since Mom died, and it was kind of sad-looking in the day. Pretty in the moonlight, though.

I don't know why I bother noticing things like that, but I do. Once I even got so worked up about the long grass growing up in the yard, those big old weeds as tall as my head, that when Dad was gone for a week or two, I cut them down myself. Only problem was, the mower was broken, and I knew Dad wouldn't want me using the sickle, so I cut that whole big yard with hedge clippers. By the time I finished the whole thing, the first part had started to grow back up again.

Now, with my eyes used to the night, I saw something move back behind the yard. The hill begins there, then slopes gentle-like, up and up. Halfway up is a big bunch of trees, and from out of that bunch is where I saw movement. Deer. They crept out of the trees, one, two, three, I counted, then five, ten about. Big ones and little ones, one with a big old head that would be full of antlers come fall.

I sat real still, not wanting to frighten them, holding my breath, willing them to come down to the yard. Don't know why, but something about deer has caught me up since I was very small — maybe because Mom loved deer. Anyway, there they came, moseying down, stopping to munch, one of them always standing still, head up, put there to guard and watch.

And then they all looked up, got stock-still, and suddenly they split apart, one going one way, one another, tails flicking white as they leapt away.

What had scared them? I knew I hadn't moved.

I looked around, tried to see what they had seen. I saw something move in the grass then, right back by the field where I'd seen it the other day — that thing I thought might be a snake. Only it was far too big, that movement there, for any snake I knew of — not even a rattlesnake or bull snake could make that kind of movement, grass waving, like creatures were in there fighting or something.

My heart began pounding hard, and I felt like I had to go see, because suddenly I began to think maybe it was Dad in that field. Maybe he was too sick to walk straight, to find his way. It had happened before that he'd staggered and fallen somewhere.

I dropped the quilt from round my shoulders, let it fall to the rocker, then stepped down off the porch.

Slowly, my heart pounding hard in my throat, I made my way down along the edge of the field. The grasses were so tall that I had to push them aside, almost as high as my waist, they were. Come summer, they'd be bigger than that, if Dad didn't come and mow them down.

I got to the edge of the field, pushed my way into the middle where the grasses still waved, but I made a lot of commotion as I went, slapping my hands against my thighs, in case it wasn't Dad, was some big snake or creature there.

Something did move then — fast, a fox, looked like, just saw its ears above the grass, or was it a coyote? Anyway, it moved and was gone, and near where it had fled, I saw what had brought it there — smelled it, too. Something on the ground, some piece of prey — something . . .

My heart lurched in my throat, because for a minute, all I could think was, *Dad*. But it wasn't Dad lying there. Just a carcass, raccoon or remains of a dead old deer, and that fox or coyote that had fled had been dining on it.

But then I heard another sound — something else, the thing that had caused the deer to flee. Human sounds.

I stood as still as the deer had, listening, my heart beating so loud that it seemed to cover every other sound. It came again, a mere whisper, the sound of twigs, earth shifting. I knew if I knelt, ear to earth, Indian style, I'd hear it even clearer, but I felt stiff, rooted. And then it came again, more clearly, footsteps, plodding slow footsteps, someone carrying something heavy.

And breathing hard. Breathing hard and humming slightly, a tuneless little sound, deep under his breath.

I turned. What to do? Hide? If it was Dad, I didn't want him to know I was out looking for him. If it wasn't Dad . . .

I looked up, saw the moon full above me, and thought, *Werewolves. Ghosts. Haunts . . .*

Foolish, that's what you are, girl, I told myself. *There's no such things as ghosts or haunts or werewolves, either. And if there are, they sure don't breathe like real people. Something else, girl: They surely don't hum.*

But I ran for the house anyway.

__Chapter 7__

I STAYED HIDDEN, crouching down below the front room window, peeking over the sill, watching, listening.

It took just moments, and then I saw it — him. Someone. Someone coming across the yard, the moonlight throwing his shadow down behind him, coming from the field where I'd just been. And whoever it was, was bent low under the weight of what he carried, tossed like a sack over his shoulder. Joseph? Dad?

Even above the call of the peepers and the night birds, I could hear the fall of his footsteps, the crackling of twigs, the soft shifting and crunching of earth beneath his feet. Then, as he got closer to the porch, I heard more humming sounds, the same sounds I'd heard before. He was breathing hard and humming under his breath.

He came closer. Came up onto the porch.

Joseph. It was Joseph. Carrying Dad?

And then Joseph was bending over, lowering his burden to the porch floor, and I saw him. Dad.

I could see his tangled reddish hair tumbling down, upside down like that as Joseph bent, could see his old overalls, his enormous feet, shoes as big as shovels.

I watched Joseph lay him down there, and I was about to show myself, open up the door, but for some reason, I held back. I felt bad somehow, like it would embarrass Dad if I went out. Embarrass me.

Anyway, I stayed back, crouching there by the windowsill, watching, hidden.

Joseph straightened up then, stood over Dad, lying there in a heap on the floor, and I could hear Joseph breathing heavy.

I held my own breath and waited for Joseph to knock. I figured in a minute, he would, and then he'd bring Dad in and lay him on the bed. But I hoped he wouldn't — would just let Dad lie there. God knows, Dad had spent many a night sleeping anywhere at all, street, fields, barroom floors, even out there on the porch. But I didn't want to see Dad this way and didn't want him to see me.

Joseph kept standing there, looking down on Dad like he was thinking, walking around in his own field of thoughts, and then he looked up at the house. Then he just shook his head, like he had debated and made a decision, didn't want to wake us up, maybe. He bent over

Dad and began straightening him out, almost like he was an undertaker, getting Dad ready for viewing. He stretched Dad's legs out straight, setting his feet side by side, then picked up each of Dad's arms, folding them gently across his chest. He was so gentle, like a woman. Next he put his hand on Dad's forehead, and I thought of a doctor checking a person for fever, but he was just pushing the hair away from Dad's face.

And then I had a scary thought, that maybe Dad was really dead! Except then I saw Dad twitch, saw his head roll a bit, and it was clear that although he was dead drunk, he was not dead.

After a bit, Joseph looked around, reached out, took the quilt from the rocking chair where I'd left it, and then he went and laid it over Dad, covering him up, right to his chin. But when he moved that quilt, there was a thump, as my notebook fell to the porch floor.

My notebook!

My heart began racing, but Joseph just picked it up and laid it back in the chair again.

Then he looked once more at Dad and went down the steps, humming softly again under his breath. And I still hadn't moved, hadn't made a sound. But I wanted to — wanted to say, *Thank you for bringing him home. I know you said you would, and you did, and I thank you.* So for the second time in just weeks, I said my thanks to him in a silent way. And hoped he knew.

Now Dad was home, asleep on our doorstep. Nothing

to do but leave him there. No sense going out, waking him, trying to get him to bed. Anyway, probably if he could be wakened, Joseph would have done it. Maybe it was because he smelled too bad, like he did sometimes when he came home, and maybe that's why Joseph had left him there — not so he wouldn't disturb us, but to let him air out kind of, to let the night air do its work on him.

And yet I had to go out there, get my notebook. Besides, I wanted to see him. See that he was all right, in one piece, not broken and . . .

Oh, he's broken all right, in the head, my voice said.

Oh, hush, I told it.

And then I settled down and waited. And waited. I waited a long time, a long, long time, till I was sure Joseph was gone, far away, out of the yard, down the hill, maybe all the way back into town.

And then, very softly, I opened the door and stepped out onto the porch.

The moonlight lay everywhere, making the porch seem to float, silvered and ghostly, throwing a white light on Dad, off to one side.

The night was warm, but as I crossed the porch, I was suddenly shivering, and I hugged my arms to myself. My feet were bare, silent on the floor, but still the boards shifted and creaked a bit under my feet. Every few steps, I'd stop, listen, hold my breath.

Don't wake up, I told him silently. Don't wake your-self. I just want to look.

For what? my voice asked.

Don't know, I answered silently.

I stood over Dad. Looked down.

My father.

Dirty matted hair. A stink — unwashed stink, sweat, beer, vomit, urine.

I moved closer, squatted on my heels beside him, knees in the air, my rear end almost touching the porch floor. I could hear his raggedly breath, see the spittle and stub-ble around his mouth. I stared hard into his face.

He twitched, a sudden movement of his shoulders and his head, and one leg came up, knee bent, then dropped sudden-like to the floor again.

I scooched back away from him, holding my breath, feeling my heart beating heavy in my throat.

Don't wake up, I prayed. *Don't.*

He stopped twitching, then moaned a little and seemed to settle back to sleep again, his breath raspy but regular.

Silently, I scooted back to him and looked at him again, stared down into his face.

Where have you been? I asked him silently. *What were you doing for twenty-two days? What do you think about when you're gone? Do you think anything at all? Do you ever think of us?*

I suddenly remembered something, something I wrote in my notebook long ago:

When you come back . . .
If you come back . . .
When you come back . . .
If you come back . . .

That's what I had written, over and over in my notebook, filled up a whole page with those words.

I sighed.

I stared at my dad for a long time, just crouched there and stared. And then suddenly I bent close, so close that I was leaning right over him, our foreheads almost touching.

"Dad?" I whispered. "Are you in there?"

He breathed at me, sour, and I backed up suddenly, losing my balance, my rear end dropping to the floor.

My heart was beating fast, tripping away like a regular old woodpecker.

Fool, my voice said. *What are you up to?*

Nothing, I answered. *Just nothing.*

Ha! she said. *You're looking for something.*

So? I said.

She laughed. *Don't look for anything from him!* she said.

Not from him, I said, angry. *Just . . . looking. Thinking.*

About what?

Don't know, I said again. *It just seems . . .*

Seems — seems like I was strangled with thoughts. About Dad, here now, off somewhere tomorrow like as not. About Will, and how he faded-like when Dad was gone.

About the ocean.

In six weeks, Mallie was going to the ocean! Could I go, now that Dad was home? Would he stay home?

I sighed. I couldn't figure it. All I knew was Dad was home. For now.

Can't figure it, I said to myself, or to the voice. *That's what I'm thinking. I'm thinking that I just can't figure it.*

__Chapter 8__

IT WAS BARELY LIGHT WHEN I WOKE, Will leaning over me, his little mouth pressed so close to me, I could feel his lips brushing my ear. "He's here!" he whispered. "Gabby, Daddy's here!"

I blinked, brushed him away from my ear. Dad? And then I remembered. Yes. He was here. I'd seen him with my own two eyes. "I know," I said. "Last night he came."

"He's asleep," Will said. "On the porch."

I nodded.

"But he'll wake up soon, right?" Will said.

"Right," I said.

I looked at the clock ticking away on the table next to the bed, squinted up my eyes at its dim, pock-marked little face. Six o'clock. Six o'clock. And today was . . . yes, Saturday! No school. I could still sleep awhile.

I turned over, aiming to go back to sleep, because God knows, there'd be plenty to deal with when I finally had to get up. "I want to sleep more," I told Will. "Go back to bed."

"I'm going out on the porch," Will said.

"Don't you bother him!" I said.

"I won't," Will answered. "But know what, Gabby?"

"What?" I said sleepily.

"When he wakes up, know what? We'll do something, him and me. Maybe he can help me with my stick people. He promised to make a barn for my horses, and then . . . Are you awake?"

"Yes, I'm awake!" I said. "Thanks to you."

"But just listen a minute!" Will said. "Remember how he told me last time about making that barn? And I got a whole lot of horses ready. I made a whole tribe — is it tribe? — no, a whole passel — I know, a *herd* of horses ready. Won't he like that?"

"Sure," I said. When he wakes up. When he sobers up. When he finally stops throwing up and can hold his head up without it breaking.

But of course I didn't say those things. Dad was home. Will was happy, would stop fading away, would start talking again.

And then I realized: He'd said more in the last five minutes than he'd said in the last two weeks!

I reached out, pulled him close to me. I squeezed him so hard, I could feel his thin little ribs pressed against my own.

"He'll like it, Will," I said. "He really will."

"I know," Will said. He wriggled away from me and slid down from the bed. I heard his footsteps go through the kitchen, then heard the screen door whine on its hinges.

I could picture him out on the porch, see him sitting beside Dad, just watching, staring at him. Waiting.

Waiting. The way we always do. Well, Dad could wait for me, too.

I turned over, pulled the covers up, fluffed my pillow, and snuggled under the quilt.

And then . . . was wide awake.

I was wide awake.

Well, fine. One day to sleep and I couldn't.

I lay for a long time, squeezing my eyes closed, waiting for sleep to come. But nothing. I was awake, wide awake. Maybe I was excited, too?

No, not excited, but surely not sleepy. Well, yes, maybe a little excited. The ocean trip. Could I go now?

May as well get up. I sat up, threw my legs over the side of the bed, and pulled on the shirt and jeans I had left lying on the floor from the day before.

I ran my hands through my hair, then went to the bathroom, brushed my teeth, and and looked at myself in the mirror.

Thin face, pointy chin, freckles. A zillion freckles. And my hair, thick and tangly and pale, no color really, except when summer comes and it gets some sun-streaks in it. About the only thing pretty about me is my eyes. They're wide and green, with little gold sparkles in them, like stars. Mom once told me I looked just like the beautiful damsel Gulnare, from the *Arabian Nights*. Mom said Gulnare looked like the damsels of the sea, and they, in turn, Mom said, are like the moon. Mom was always reading, reading and telling me stories. She said the damsels were beautiful, just like me, and that they could walk upon the surface of the water. And when I asked her how a damsel — a girl — could walk on water, she looked at me with that wide-eyed way she had, so much like the way Will looks at times, and said, "Why, Gabrielle, *all* girls can do whatever they aim to do."

When I said I didn't believe her, she just smiled, and said, "You'll see someday, Gabrielle. Just remember what I said."

And I had. I'd remembered it all those years. But I still didn't see how it could be. And I could see for sure I wasn't beautiful.

I sighed and looked around the bathroom. That room would smell for days to come — he'd be in there throwing up, leaving his stink.

I shook my head and went out to the kitchen.

I looked through the screen door to the porch, saw Will sitting beside Dad, still stretched out there on the floor, the quilt thrown off now, one arm thrown up across his shaggy head.

Will saw me looking, smiled at me, then turned back to stare down at Dad. Waiting.

I turned, went to the stove, and started up some coffee.

Well, the good was, he was home, maybe long enough this time to earn some money, buy some stuff we sorely needed, like shoes for Will — his were almost worn through, and by fall, he'd surely need new ones. Best to get them now, or as soon as Dad got some money, buy them too big, make sure he'd have them when he needed them. And a coat, too. And new pants. The old ones were worn thin, but funny, Will didn't seem to outgrow any-thing, not much, anyway. Other boys his age shot up like weeds, but Will was a slow grower.

So we'd get clothes, and we'd get food. Maybe I'd even get a new notebook. This time, when Dad took us to town, I'd take over the food shopping, get stuff we really needed because sometimes Dad bought dumb kinds of things that nobody would eat — like the time he brought home snails — snails in a can! To eat! I'd buy bacon and eggs and peanut butter and bread and cereal and canned things that last, things like tuna fish and canned spaghetti and pickles maybe, Will loves pickles, and spaghetti sauce and . . . I took a deep breath. And be ready for the next time that he left.

And . . . and . . . could I go to the ocean? Could I? He was home. Maybe I could. Maybe . . .

I hadn't told Will about the trip — why worry him? He'd pester and bother me, telling me I should go every chance he had. I had to decide this on my own.

But now? Maybe?

Maybe not, my voice said.

Maybe, I answered silently. *Don't know. Dad does love Will. So he'd be good to him. And Will loves him so much, he practically adores him. But —*

But you can't count on him, my voice said.

I turned, looked at Will out there on the porch, looking down at Dad. Still waiting. I nodded. Yes, even if Dad stayed awhile, even if he promised to stay with Will while I was gone, even so, he might pick up and go.

I sighed. *No,* I said. *You can't. You can't count on him.*

Can't count on anything, my voice answered.

＿Chapter 9＿

But about that, my voice was wrong. I could count on one thing — that Dad would be sweet and humble once he came to. He was always like that when he first came back, always. I remember that from as long ago as when Mom was still alive. Dad would come back looking shy and a little ashamed, and he always brought flowers for Mom, flowers tied up with a ribbon, which he held behind his back.

Mom, she wouldn't look right at him, I remember that, always looked away when he'd first come in, like maybe she didn't want to see him, or couldn't bear for him to see her face. But she took his flowers all right, and after a while, she'd look up and smile at him. And then she'd tell us, Will and me — and him — that he was a good man.

Now, though, it took him a while to wake up, come to. When he finally did, he tumbled into the house, holding on to the walls and the door frames, not speaking, not looking at us, not looking at anything but the floor, and then he disappeared into the bathroom. He was there for hours. Just hours and hours. I even think he fell asleep in there, he was so still, but neither me nor Will wanted to knock and disturb him. And then, after a long time, we heard the water running in the tub and for the longest time, it ran and ran and ran. The well would be empty if he kept that up!

Will and I waited, sitting at the kitchen table, sat there half the morning and into the afternoon, our eyes fixed on that bathroom door. Don't know why we sat there — maybe needed to see if he'd come out alive, I expect.

Anyway, another long time went by, and then finally the bathroom door opened and at last, he showed himself.

He stood there, leaning against the door frame, then raised a hand to us, both of us sitting there formal-like at that table as if we were a welcoming committee, like they have at church for newcomers.

"Hello?" he said. It was tentative the way he said it, and the look in his eyes was worried.

"Daddy!" Will said. "Sit by me!"

He jumped up, scooted over to Dad, and took him by the hand.

Dad let Will take his hand, let Will lead him across the

room to the table. I noticed that Dad moved slowly, carefully, lifting each foot high, then setting it down cautiously, almost like he was blind or something.

Will led Dad to a chair at the table and stood by him while he eased himself down into it.

Dad breathed deeply awhile, laid his head back against the chair, his breath coming in quick spurts, panting almost, like he'd walked miles instead of just a few steps. "You're a good helper, Will," Dad said when he finally seemed able to speak. "You always are."

Will blinked, ducked his head, then looked over at me. "Gabby's a good helper, too," he said.

Dad didn't answer, didn't look at me, either.

But I looked at him. His hair was washed, his face clean and shaved, but full of nicks and little bleeding places with bits of tissue stuck to them. He had put on different clothes, took them from the bathroom rack where he kept his work clothes and yard clothes, but still, he smelled a bit.

The lines in his face looked deeper than they used to look, but maybe they weren't, maybe it was just that I hadn't seen him in so long, I'd forgotten. His eyes — I couldn't really see his eyes, seeing as how he was looking down. But under his eyes, there was dark skin, puffy and swollen.

"You hungry?" Will said. "We could make you something to eat, eggs or something. Gabby's been making good things."

"No," Dad said. He scrunched up his face, put one hand on his middle as if there was a pain there. "Nothing to eat now."

"Daddy?" Will said.

"What, Will?"

"Now that you're home, will you help me make a horse barn? Remember, like you said?"

"I said that?" Dad said. He put his hands on the table, his fingers splayed out, then scrunched up his face and frowned down at them, like he'd never seen them before.

"You said," Will said. "And now you're home, you will, right?"

Dad didn't answer. He just kept frowning at his hands. Then, after a minute, he began lifting his fingers, one, then another, up, then down. He kept on doing that, lifting each one, slowly, carefully, one at a time, up, then down, like he was testing to see if they were working or not.

Eventually he drew a deep breath. "You said something, Will," Dad said. "Now that I'm home, you said?"

"Yes," Will said. "Now that you're home, will you?"

Dad didn't look up from his fingers. "I guess I've been gone awhile?" he said.

Awhile? How about twenty-two days? Is that enough of a while? But I didn't say anything.

"Yeah," Will said. "But you're back now."

"How long?" Dad said.

Will didn't answer for a minute. Neither did I. Let Dad figure it out if he really wanted to.

I watched Will look down at the floor, watched him curl and uncurl his bare toes around the rungs of his chair. "Awhile," Will said softly. "Twenty-two days."

"That long?" Dad said. He shook his head, then put a hand to it, like he was in pain. "I guess you were wondering, eh?"

"I wasn't," Will said. "I knew you'd come back. But Gabby . . . Gabby got mad."

"I did not!" I said, glaring at Will. "You say the dumbest things!"

"Could hardly blame you if you were mad," Dad said. The first thing he'd said to me. Although he still didn't look at me.

"Well, I wasn't," I said. And I have no idea why I said that. I'd been plenty mad. Still was.

But why talk about it? Whether I was mad or not mad, sad or not sad, he'd still do whatever it was he was going to do. Besides, he was home now. What was the sense of spoiling today with what had happened yesterday?

I couldn't help thinking, though, that I better remind Will not to get too excited, remind him how this was just temporary, that Dad would be gone again. Eventually. Here today, gone tomorrow. He'd go again. He always did.

"Gabrielle?" Dad said, his voice soft.

I felt this skip inside my chest, my heart doing this

dumb thumping it does at times — times like this, when Dad calls me by my whole name, just the way Mom used to do. Like he means something special by saying that. Like I'm something special.

"Gabrielle?" Dad said again, and he looked up at me.

"What?" I said.

Dad took a deep breath, slow and shaky. "Know what, Gabrielle?" he said. "You look so much like your mother sometimes."

I didn't answer.

"I won't go away again," Dad said. "Promise."

But you will go away again. You always do.

"Gabby's going on a vacation," Will said. "Now that you're home. With Mallie and her brother, Les, and their mom and dad. They're going to see the ocean, right after school's over. Gabby's always wanted to see the ocean, right, Gabby?"

I just stared at him. The ocean? I hadn't told him a thing about going to the ocean, about Mallie's invitation, not anything!

Like he knew what I was thinking, he said, "Les told me. He said you were invited, but not me, but that's all right. It's just because they have room for just one person and Mallie's the oldest, so she got to invite somebody."

"Are you, Gabrielle?" Dad said. "Really? That's great! We'll go to town, get you some new clothes and —"

"No!" I said, my heart suddenly lurching, the racing

feeling so bad I thought it would leap right out of my chest. "I don't need anything, not any new clothes or anything. Just if you could stay here with Will . . ."

I couldn't believe I had blurted that out! How could I? I felt like running, hiding, just like I used to when I was little. Fool that I was. Like Dad would stay!

Like he was reading my mind, he looked up at me, and I looked back. His eyes were tired, red and heavy-lidded, but I could see he was trying to smile. "Promise," he said. He put a hand to his chest and made a little *X* sign, just like kids do at school. "I promise."

I shrugged, looked away.

"You wait and see," Dad said.

I just shook my head.

"Gabby?" Will said. He was looking at me, a pleading kind of look. "Daddy means it."

I nodded. Dad did mean it. I knew that. But then Dad always meant it.

Chapter 10

NEXT MORNING, SUNDAY MORNING, I showered, fixed my hair, got all ready for Sunday school, then went to get Will ready. It was still early, but already he was out on the porch with Dad, both of them working on the horse barn. There were sticks and twigs and bits of shingle, all sorts of stuff spread out on the floor in front of them.

Their heads were together, and neither looked up when I came out onto the porch; they were so absorbed, they didn't even hear me.

I just stood watching a minute, listening to Will's constant chatter as he moved one stick, then another, laying out the whole structure, leaning back a bit to check it out, then bending back in close.

With their heads pressed together like that, I could see

how alike their hair was — Dad's tinged with gray, but still that golden color, shot through with bits of red, Will's a bit more golden, like sunlight when it fades into sunset, or like . . .

Like it was something I wanted to write about, how alike they were, how like . . . but did I want to write about Dad? Put him in my notebook? Mostly I tried to keep him out of my writings, although lately he'd had a way of sneaking in, just the way he snuck into my dreams.

"Come on, Will," I said. "Time to get ready for Sunday school."

Will turned, looked up at me. "Oh, Gabby!" he said. "Do I have to? I don't want to go. Please!" He turned back to Dad, leaned against him. "Daddy?" he said, looking up into Dad's face. "Daddy, tell her I don't have go, please?"

But Dad just shook his head, didn't answer.

Will turned to me again, his big eyes wide. "Just this once Gabby," he said, folding his hands together like he was praying. "Just for today. I'll pray right here at home. Promise."

"Will!" I said. I put my fists on my hips, looked from him to Dad.

Dad, though, he just kept his head bent over the twigs, moving sticks from one place to another, holding his head to one side, as though picturing where each one would go in the building, then bending again to move another stick or twig. He seemed really intent on his work, although I could tell he was listening. I even had a feeling he was smiling.

"Gabby?" Will said. "I'll pray. I promise. And God . . . He won't mind. It will be okay with Him."

"How do you know it's okay with Him?" I said severely. "You shouldn't say things like that."

Will shrugged, looked down at his hands, then up at me, his lower lip jutting out. "Pastor says you can know what God wants."

"By reading your Bible," I said. "Not by pretending that God wants what you want."

I stood there, hands on hips, glaring at him. And then I thought: Why was I playing this fool part? I wasn't at all sure about God myself, wasn't even sure God cared if Will went or not. The only reason I did this church thing was for Will.

I shrugged. "Fine!" I said. "Stay home. See if I care."

I turned, went back in the house, grabbed my prayer book, the went down the path to wait for Mallie.

It was just a little while before Mallie came flying down her drive, dancing and whirling around and around, in that wild way she has.

As soon as she saw me, she grabbed my arm, hugged tight, then whirled me around, too. "Where's Will?" she said. "No, don't tell me, I know, he's with your dad. So say yes. Right now. Say yes you can come with us on our vacation. I know he's home."

I didn't answer. I wasn't surprised she knew he was home. In this town, there aren't any secrets.

"Say it!" she said again.

I smiled, couldn't help it, the way she was so excited-like. "Maybe," I said.

She stopped whirling. "Oh, wow! That means yes. *Maybe* always means yes!"

"Uh-uh," I said, glaring at her. "*Maybe* means maybe!"

She shrugged. "I don't believe you. So listen, guess what? My dad hired this camper thing, and we're going to pull it along behind the car. We went out to see it on the rental lot yesterday. It's so cool. Inside the camper, there's this tiny sink and a little stove and at night, beds fold out of the walls — they're part of the benches and the table. But guess what, best of all? We're taking a tent, and you and me, we can have the tent all to ourselves, so we don't have to sleep with Les or my mom and dad, we can have the whole tent to ourselves, unless you're scared of bears — oh, are you scared of bears? I guess I am, too, but I don't think there are any bears, not really, I mean, not in the —"

She stopped and looked at me. "How come you're not excited?" she said. "You haven't said a word."

"How could I?" I said. "You haven't stopped talking."

"Oh," she said. "Well, your turn. I won't say a word. Only, look at that . . ."

She pointed.

"What?" I said.

"That. That bird," she whispered.

I looked where she was pointing, saw this bird, this tiny, perfect little bluebird. We both stood still, watching it for a moment. I hadn't seen a bluebird in years, yet hardly anyone seemed to know why they'd disappeared. Mama used to call them birds of God, said God had let them loose from heaven for us. This one was perched on a fence by the field, a breeze ruffling it a bit, causing the tiny pinkish feathers on its breast to lift and settle, lift and settle, but its little face seemed scrunched up, almost as if it was frowning.

"Isn't it adorable?" Mallie said. "Don't you wish that God made us like birds, I mean, like we had wings and could fly, not that I'd want to have feathers, and they say that birds' brains are really small, so they're probably pretty dumb. And know what else? I heard that birds get mites, that's those little buglike things, sort of like fleas, and you'd itch so —"

I was just looking at her, my arms folded.

She clapped a hand over her mouth. "I won't say another word," she whispered from behind her hand, but I could see she was grinning. "Promise."

"I don't believe it," I said.

She kept her hand on her mouth, shook her head.

We started walking again, headed into town and church, walking side by side, close, not speaking for a while.

Finally I said, "I don't know. I can't trust him. I know

he means it when he says he'll stay. But he always goes off again anyway."

"He's home," she said. "That's what matters."

"But suppose he leaves Will alone when I'm gone?"

"He won't," she said. "He knows Will's too little to leave alone. Anyway, how does he seem now? I mean, like how does he act?"

"Tired," I said. "Sick. But know what? This morning he was out there with Will, the two of them playing together like nothing was wrong, like everything was the same, like he'd never been gone, like he was always here."

"Maybe this time he won't go," she said.

I didn't bother to answer that.

She was quiet for so long that I began to smile. But I knew it wouldn't last. So I just waited, and after a minute, she spoke, but when she did, she sounded quiet, thoughtful.

"Gabby?" she said. "Know what I was thinking?"

"What?" I said.

"I was thinking about God," she answered. "Do you believe God answers prayers?"

I looked at her. "Do you?" I said.

"Yes," she said. "I think so. And I'm going to pray, I'm going to pray like anything. I might even get other people to pray with me, like a prayer circle."

"Don't you do it!" I said, grabbing her by the arm. "Don't you dare tell —"

"I'm not telling," she said, shaking off my hand. "People won't have to know what they're praying for, just that they're praying for something incredibly special."

I shrugged.

"You don't believe it works, do you?" she said.

"It can't hurt," I said. "I guess."

"It works," she said. "I know it does."

I took a deep breath, looked away.

Maybe it would work. Maybe Dad would stay put. But long enough to let me go? Long enough to care for Will? Long enough to stay with Will while I was gone? Could I trust him to do that?

I sighed. It was so confusing. I mean, how could you learn to trust? When you'd already learned not to?

__Chapter 11__

SUMMER WEATHER WAS SUDDENLY ON US — the days hot, nights hot too, and school would be over soon — and Dad was still at home. He seemed better each day, more clear in his head, although he didn't seem all that steady on his feet, like maybe the drink had made him dizzy inside. Yet he'd been home three whole weeks, and he hadn't slipped off to Dally's even once. Did that mean anything?

Also, the longer he stayed and the better he got, the better Will got, too, more talkative, more playful, more — hungry! He ate like anything, and I think he even gained weight, began to fill out a little so his ribs didn't stick out so much. And funny, but he also got to be more of a pain. He argued with me about everything, argued about bedtimes, hated taking baths, wouldn't go to church without Dad, answered back when I told him to do things. He got real feisty, and yet — this was hard to explain, even to myself, but there it was — somehow I liked him better this way. Maybe it was because he seemed more like a real boy instead of a shadow. Still, there were times I'd have cheerfully wrung his neck — like when he ignored me about playing in the woodpile or when he gave me that wide-eyed look and swore he had taken a bath, when you could see he still had all the day's dirt on him, and the tub wasn't even wet!

He was better, though, and that was the most important thing. There was another important thing that happened: Dad got work. It's never hard for Dad to do since he's so good with his hands, and there's always work in the warm weather for someone who wants to pick crops or cut hay or tend to repairs. But this time, he got good work — at the mill, cutting lumber, something he was good at, with his hands so quick and so trained to the feel of wood — probably that's where Will's talent came from. I did worry, though. Each day, around sunset, I worried — waiting, waiting for him to come home. Would he come home this time? Or would he go straight into town, straight to the bar?

But he did come home. Every single day. Three weeks, twenty-one days now, and he'd come home every single day. And each day that went by, I thought more and more about the trip to the ocean, wondered about it, wondered about trusting Dad.

And then, on the twenty-second day, something happened, something I thought might never happen. We had been sitting at supper, and I'd noticed Dad looking at me. Every time I looked up, he was watching me.

"Gabrielle?" Dad said. "I'm not leaving again. It's a promise. I want you to believe that."

"I know that, Dad," I said. "I believe you." Because what else could I say?

"Good," Dad said, and then he smiled. "Now I have a surprise for you," he said. "For both of you."

I just looked back. I wasn't keen on any surprises from him.

"What, Daddy?" Will said.

"It's this," Dad said. He took an envelope out of his pocket. "I wrote to Clara. Your grandma. Your great-grandma. I told her we want to come visit, and she wrote back. She'd like us to come next Saturday. I'm going to borrow Joseph's pickup truck and we'll all go."

"Oh, wow!" Will squealed. "A truck! We get to ride in a truck!" He was jumping up and down in his chair, so excited.

Me, I just squinted up my eyes at Dad. "Why?" I said.

"Why what?" Dad answered.

"Why are we going?" I asked.

Dad just shrugged.

"I thought you didn't like her," I said.

"I like her all right!" Dad said. "We just . . . have had our differences, that's all."

I just looked at him, puzzled. If he hadn't liked her before, didn't like for her to come visit us and we didn't visit her — why should we want to go see her now?

Yet a part of me was pleased. At least now I'd be able to picture her, find out if she was any good in an emergency in case we needed her. And a part of me was just plain curious.

"Oh, Daddy!" Will said. "What color is his truck? Is it that red one?"

Dad turned to Will. "Yes, it's the red one," he said. And that's all the two of them talked about for the rest of the week — the truck and how wonderful it would be to ride in it.

When that Saturday finally came, Dad had himself all washed and slicked up, and he made me and Will put on our best things — he wanted me to wear a skirt — and off we went. I have to admit that riding in the pickup was fun. It must be nice to have a car or truck of your own, nice to feel you can just go off somewhere, nothing to tie you down.

All the way, Will was just beside himself excited, bouncing up and down on the seat between me and Dad. He wasn't just excited about the truck. He seemed to have decided that having a granny or great-granny was the best thing that had ever happened to him — maybe from reading books about nice old grannies or something, Lord knows. Me, I was just plain curious.

It was a fine morning to be going anywhere, the sun bright, the air clear and hot, and we left the windows in the truck down, let the wind blow in. The roads out that way are all bumpy and rough, and Will kept squealing with delight every time we hit a bump and got all jiggled up. We drove for about an hour — that would be maybe ten or twelve hours walking. (I always thought about that kind of thing — how long it would take to walk — seeing as how I might need to make that trip with Will someday.) And then, after all that time, we turned onto a small narrow path, and Dad had to put the truck in a different gear, and it wheezed its way up, up a hilly ridge, rutted out with rain and years of cars maybe making their way up there, a long, long hill up. And then, after climbing for what seeemed forever, jouncing and bumping, the road ended abruptly in a small clearing, and we were there. Dad pulled up and stopped, turned off the engine, and we all sat, just looking.

It suddenly seemed so quiet — no rumbling of the truck, no wind in our ears. All I could hear were crickets and cicadas jabbering, and an old bullfrog clunking out his sounds. A hawk circled above us, its wing tips edged with the morning light, circling round and round, as if it were looking down at us, and at the small metal trailer that was Clara's home.

None of us moved to get out, just sat, taking it all in for a few minutes. The trailer was rusted in spots, looking a bit like an overgrown tin can. There was chicken wire covering the door, with netting nailed to it to keep out flies. Beside the trailer, on a little platform covered with a tiny shedlike roof, was a washing machine.

Hanging from a tree in front, hung by ropes slung over some heavy branches, was an engine, probably a truck engine, because behind it stood this huge old yellow pickup truck, as yellow as a lemon, its hood up, its guts missing.

There were some faded green folding chairs tilted crazy-like against the trailer, and around the corner, just visible, was a sink lying on its side, and the skeleton of a rusted-out car.

But funny thing was, it wasn't all that ugly — well, maybe it was a little messy, but it wasn't as homely as it could have been — because all around there were flowers, flowers everywhere you looked, beautiful flowers. They were in window boxes; they were planted in an old bathtub; there was a big bunch of marigolds planted inside a huge old truck tire. In the middle of the yard, there was this iron thing — reminded me of this huge twisted stork with one foot up and its wings out — and hanging from its wings and pulled-up leg, there were more pots of flowers.

There were pink geraniums, and blue and purple petunias and orange marigolds, and other kinds of flowers that I didn't recognize, zillions of colors, none of them matching or even blending, wild-looking, like somebody had thrown down handfuls of any old seeds and they had caught on. And of course, bluebonnets — everywhere, wild and sassy, those beautiful blue flowers. It was very, very pleasing, at least to me, haphazard and wild like that.

"This is it, Daddy?" Will said, his voice small, quiet, hushed the way you get in church.

"This is it, son," Dad said.

"Where's Clara?" Will said.

"She's probably inside," Dad said. "Or back in her garden."

"You said she had no dog, right?" Will said.

"No dog," Dad said, smiling and putting a hand on Will's knee. And I wondered how Dad knew there was no dog.

"Is this where you grew up?" Will said.

Dad shook his head. "No. We lived in town when I was little. Granny moved out here when she met her husband, Jake. He's gone now."

"Gone?" Will whispered, turning to Dad, worried looking.

Dad gave him a quick look. "Dead," he said.

"Oh," Will said.

"Well, are you going to sit there all day?" a voice called, and I could see a figure looming just inside the open doorway, behind the chicken wire and screens.

Dad looked over at Will and me. "Sounds like her," he said, grinning.

Then he opened his door and jumped to the ground, more lively-looking than I'd seen him in ages. I opened my door, too, and got out, and Will slid to the ground beside me. Will had become shy again, and he reached for my hand, squeezing it tight.

"Come in, come on!" she called, and she held the door wide. "Don't just stand there, get yourselves in here!"

We crossed the yard, Dad first, then me, leading Will, who was pulling back on my hand, like he did on the first day of school.

Inside, it took a minute for my eyes to adjust to the lack of light, to see details clear, but you didn't need much to see this: This was the biggest woman I had ever seen. I had forgotten how tall she was. She must have been six feet tall — as tall as Dad — and she was wide. I mean, huge. She wore jeans and a man's plaid shirt, the tails hanging down around her, and when I could see details clear enough, I saw that her hands were dirty, dirt under her fingernails and in the ridges of her knuckles, like the hands of people who work in garages.

Her hair wasn't white and it wasn't gray, but a kind of silvery color, like coyote fur, and it was twisted into a long braid that hung down her back, and in her ears were long, dangly earrings of turquoise and silver.

She didn't look at or even speak to Will and me — just moved in close to Dad and stood there eyeing him, looking him up and down.

For a long time she stared at him, and I couldn't help

noticing that Dad was acting like boys do at school when they're being stared down by the teacher. He met her eyes, but then he looked away, then back, then away again, like he didn't want to look at her but was forcing himself to meet her eyes.

While they looked each other over, I looked around the trailer. I'd never been in one before, and I was curious. It didn't look that different from a regular house, though — just smaller. And it was dark, Lord, it was dark in there, everything brown — carpet, sofa, paneled fake wood walls, hardly any windows, and the ones there were, were dusty. But again there were bits of plants and flowers everywhere, on the sink, on the windowsill over the sink, on the floors and the kitchen table, two or three of them with little lights aimed at them.

One thing I did see, right next to the sofa — a telephone, and on the little round circle in the middle, the telephone number. I instantly memorized that number, said it over and over in my head, till I had it down. You could never tell.

I looked again at Dad and Clara. They were still looking each other over, so still and watchful that I half expected them to start circling each other, the way stray cats do that meet up in a barn. But after a minute, Clara reached over and touched Dad lightly on the arm. "You're here," she said quietly. "That's what counts."

And then she turned to face me and Will.

"You're Gabby," she said, fixing her eyes on me. "You sure have shot up. And that there's Will."

"Yes, ma'am," I answered. And suddenly felt as shy as Will.

"Call me Clara," she said. "How old are you?"

"Twelve," I answered. "Twelve going on thirteen."

"Lord! A woman practically!" Clara nodded at Will. "And what about him? How old is he now?"

I pushed Will forward a little. "Tell her," I said.

Will just shook his head, staring at the ground. He reached for my hand again, held it tight.

"Will!" I poked him. "Tell her."

He didn't answer.

I just shook my head, gave up on him. "He's six," I said. "Will is six."

"Small for six," Clara said.

Will looked up suddenly. "I build things," he whispered.

I looked at him, surprised. He hardly ever volunteers anything.

"You build things?" Clara said. "What kind of things?"

"Just . . . things," Will said, just a little louder.

"Big things, little things, what kinds of things?" she said again.

Will reached in the pocket of his pants.

Carefully he drew out a small, folded package. He

sat down then, cross-legged on the floor, and began to unwrap it. It was wrapped in tissues, toilet tissue. He turned it over and over till all the tissue was off, then held it up.

It was one of his stick men — a stick man riding a horse.

I wish I could describe exactly how good he does, but I never can — maybe because I'm not an artist like him — but it was pretty incredible, sticks and twigs with bits of wire or string, bits of magic. There was motion in the horse's legs, and the man was leaning forward, holding tight to the horse's back, like they were flying in the wind, and you could almost see the wind fly through the horse's mane, pulling the mane back, the man's hair back, the hat on his head tipped back with the wind.

Clara put her hand out flat, palm up, and Will laid the figure on her hand.

For a long minute, she looked at it, not saying anything. And then she looked at Will, then back again at the figure, and then over at Dad.

She turned back to Will again, put her hand out, the figure still lying there on her palm, the wind blowing at it still, held it out for him to take back. "Beautiful," she said. "An artist like your pa."

Dad was an artist? Well, yes, I guess, the way he worked with his hands, the way he was so good with wood.

"You can keep it if you like," Will said quietly.

Her eyebrows went up.

"You can," Will said. "I have others."

She looked down at the little figure and smiled. And then she turned, went over to the sink, and placed the figure carefully on the windowsill there, where she had all her plant cuttings and pots and stuff. "You'll like it there," she said softly, as if she was talking right to the man and his horse. "It's nice and sunny. And you can watch me while I work."

__Chapter 12 __

THE WHOLE MORNING WAS AWKWARD-LIKE, at least for me, and I could tell for Dad, too. Dad just sat on the edge of the sofa or wandered around the room, stiff as if he was at a wake, his eyes narrowed, worried-looking, glancing around like he was wondering what in the world he had done bringing us here and how we were going to get out. And me, I wondered the same thing. I felt awkward, sitting there, hands in lap like I was a choir girl or something. I hadn't even thought to bring a book with me or anything, don't know why I hadn't thought of that. And I wished like anything that I had my notebook, not that I'd probably write right there, but maybe I could have taken it out back or something.

But Will — well, he and Clara got on like anything, talking back and forth about Will's stick figures, about flowers and food, even about cars, like they were two old friends. Everybody likes Will, and I'm never quite sure why, with him so quiet and shy. Mostly I'm happy, though, when they like him — Lord knows, he has a hard enough life, so it's good to have people take a shine to him. But this time, don't know why, I felt sort of jealous. I wanted to say to Clara, talk to me, I'm a person, too. But of course I didn't. So she just banged around her trailer house, dumping out tin cans of soil and sticking in new plant cuttings, and talking to Will, who followed her around puppy-like, and then talking to Dad, and asking him questions about us and telling him about things I didn't know anything about — like neighbor things and things about when he was a child.

Suddenly she seemed to notice me. "Hungry?" she said abruptly.

I nodded. "I guess," I said.

"Then, come on," she said.

She stopped with the plant cuttings and began taking out makings for lunch — bread and peanut butter and jam and fruit.

I went to help, and she gave me a pitcher to make up some tea, and at least then I felt like I had a job to do, something besides sitting like a statue.

When Clara had the sandwiches ready, she handed me a blanket to take outside and spread it out. We'd eat on the ground out there, which was fine with me.

I laid out the blanket, taking my time so I could enjoy

the outside by myself a minute. But in about another minute, they had all come out, and we sat down to eat, Will taking a place between Clara and Dad on the blanket.

When we had all settled down and taken a sandwich, Clara looked around, up at the sky. "Going to storm by nightfall," she said. "Got to cover up that engine." She looked over at the engine hanging from ropes on the tree.

I looked where she looked, then looked up at the sky — clear blue, just the faintest streaks of clouds, the sun shining so hot it was fierce almost, a breeze ruffling the leaves on the trees.

Didn't look like any storm brewing to me.

"Don't believe me, do you?" she said, looking at me, reading my mind, it seemed.

I shrugged. "Just doesn't look that way to me," I said.

"See the leaves turning over, upside down like that?" she said.

I looked at the trees. The leaves were being lightly tossed, turning over, their silver undersides showing as they flipped into the breeze.

"Going to storm when the leaves show their petticoats," she said. "And see the streaky clouds?" She tilted her head up, poked her chin at the sky. "Same thing — storm on the way. How old did you say you were? Twelve?"

"Thirteen, almost," I said.

"Learn to read the signs," she said.

"Gabby loves outdoors," Will said suddenly. "She's going to the ocean."

"I am not!" I said.

"You are, too," Will said. He looked at Clara. "Gabby's going with her best friend. Gabby loves the ocean."

I looked down, could feel myself blushing. Don't know why, but it seemed like Will was telling my business, my private, personal business. And anyway, how could he say for sure I was going when I didn't even know? But Lord, how I wished I could. And thought again how well Dad had been doing, how he hadn't slipped off to Dally's even once.

I took a quick look at Dad, wondering if he had remembered about Mallie, about the invitation, but he didn't seem to be listening. He was just staring at the trailer, eyes squinted up like he was studying it.

"Ever been to the ocean?" Clara asked.

She was looking right at me, her clear gray eyes wide. I was surprised how clear they were — not like an old lady's at all, although the skin around them was kind of wrinkled up.

"No," I said. "Never."

"I've been," Clara said. "It's something to see."

"Did you like it?" I asked.

She nodded. "Well, 'course I like the country round here better. But yes, I liked it. Winds and waves and flowers — sea grasses. And birds!"

"I can make a bird," Will said, looking up at her. "Want me to make you one? I can make big ones or little ones."

"After lunch," Clara said. She pointed a finger at him. "But I'll tell you something — some of those shore birds, they were as big as you. You need to fatten up some. Little birds, they don't stand a chance. At the ocean, I'd watch little birds fly into the wind, and the wind would push them right back again. Push the waves, too. What a racket it all made!"

"A racket?" I said.

She nodded. "Not quiet like here," she said. "The ocean's a noisy place."

I looked down at my sandwich, frowning. Mom had said the ocean whispered, and sometimes, she said, it sounds like the wind in the wheat fields, gray waves of wheat, rustling in the wind. And Gabrielle, sometimes the moon hangs so close over the ocean, that there seem to be twin moons and . . .

I looked up. Clara was looking at me, her eyebrows up. "What?" she said.

"Nothing," I said. "It's just that Mom said . . ."

I paused, looked at Dad, at Will.

Will was picking stems off of grapes, and Dad, he was still staring off at the trailer.

I looked back at Clara. "My mother," I said. "She said the ocean whispers."

Clara nodded a few times, slowly, slowly. And then

after a minute, she said, "Yes. Yes, your mama was right. Sometimes the ocean does whisper."

I took a deep breath. "That's what she said," I said, and for some reason, felt relieved.

"And when you've seen it," Clara went on. "You come back and tell me about it."

I looked away. If I went.

"Know what?" Will said suddenly. "I like the name Clara."

She looked at him, smiled.

She reached out then, lay one finger on his cheek for just a moment before she drew it back, and she looked over at me at the same time.

I quick looked away, could feel myself blushing. How come I felt jealous?

I bent my head over my sandwich. It was just peanut butter and jelly, but it was good — on thick, white bread, and the jam was strawberry — homemade strawberry.

"The jam is good," I said quickly, looking for something to say, some way to make her stop looking at me.

"I remember when your granny used to make this strawberry jam," Dad said, speaking up for the first time. "Used to make the whole place steam up like anything. Couldn't even see out the kitchen windows."

"That was back at the house," Clara said. "Big old place. Never missed it once I left, though. Too much to take care of."

"Home, though," Dad said quietly.

"That it was," she said. "For a while."

"Where was it, Dad?" I said.

"Out Route Sixty-six just" — he looked up, frowned at the sky — "six miles from here? Seven?"

"About," Clara said.

"Was it nice, Dad?" I said. "Did you like that house?"

Dad just shrugged. "It was all right." He took a bite of his sandwich.

"Is the house still there?" I asked.

Dad chewed slowly, swallowed, then picked up his glass of tea, and drank it all the way down. "Probably," he said finally. "But maybe not. I haven't been there in . . . what? Twenty, twenty-five years? Long before you were born. Seems a shame, but that's the way it is." He sighed. "Things change. People change."

"That they do," Clara daid.

Something about her voice made me look at her, and I saw Will look at her, too.

Dad didn't look, though.

There was a long silence while Dad shook his head slowly, like shaking away a sad thought.

"Dad?" I said.

He didn't answer.

"Do you miss it, Dad?" I asked. "How old were you when you moved here?"

"I didn't move here," he said. "I just left. Got all grown up and left."

"Oh," I said.

"Wrong," Clara said. "You weren't grown up."

Dad just shrugged. "I was fifteen," he said. "That was grown up enough."

"You left home when you were fifteen?" I said. I stared at him.

Dad nodded. "Why not?" he said. "I was big for my age. Nobody knew. Besides, I was close to sixteen."

"But Dad!" I said.

"What?" he said. He looked at me, his eyebrows up, a little twist to his mouth that looked like maybe it was a smile. Except maybe it wasn't. "What?" he said again.

I just shook my head, didn't say the rest of what I was thinking: You were just a kid. You were just a little older than me! How could you live on your own?

Will and me, we were alone a lot. But at least we had a house to live in.

I looked from him to Clara. How could she let him go — at fifteen? Didn't she ever try to find him, bring him back? She was looking at me, her clear gray eyes fixed right on me.

"It was Jake," she said. "He just couldn't stand Jake, couldn't stand the thought of having another papa. One who laid down some rules."

Dad didn't look up, but a red flush suddenly spread up his neck. "He wasn't my papa," he said.

"Could have been," she said. "He tried to be. Tried like anything to keep you from that wild crowd with their wild antics. All that business."

"History," Dad said with a shrug. And then after a minute, he took a deep breath and he said, very softly, "It wouldn't have made any difference."

Nobody spoke for a while. And then Will said, "Daddy?"

Dad looked at him.

"What'd you do then?" Will said. "I mean, after you were fifteen, after you left home? Who took care of you? Did you have money?"

Will looked so anxious, so worried-like, that for a minute, I wanted to reach over and touch him, to tell him it was all right. But then I felt exasperated. Will can be such a baby sometimes. Dad had made it, had survived.

But I guess Dad had the same feeling I had, the first feeling, not the exasperated one, because he reached over and touched Will lightly on the head. "I found a way," he said quietly. "Look at me. I found a way."

"If you can call it that," Clara said.

Dad turned to her. "Yes, I call it that," he said. "I do." He stood up and brushed the crumbs off his pants. Then he looked down at Clara and smiled, a tiny, soft kind of smile but sad, too. "I found a way, and it works for me," he repeated softly. "No matter what you think."

__Chapter 13__

ALL THE WAY HOME THAT NIGHT, we were silent, even though for the first little while, I tried to get Dad to talk.

What was he thinking? Why was he so quiet? I hated when he got too quiet-like. It meant that another bout was coming on him, the bout of the quiet times. They always came just before the other times, his off times.

And there were just two weeks left before the trip to the ocean!

I didn't care what Dad talked about — Clara, about the trailer house, the strawberry jam, about the old house, anything, just to keep him from sinking into that silence that I could see creeping over him. But all he'd do was shake his head, and once I guess I had asked one thing too much, because he seemed annoyed with me, something he hardly ever is. "Don't bother your head about history, Gabby!" he said.

"But Dad?" I said.

"No," he said.

"Just one thing?" I said.

He took a deep breath. "What?" he said.

I took a deep breath myself. "Just wondering," I said. "I mean, I was wondering why we went to see Clara? I mean, why now?"

"Why not?" Dad said.

And that was that. He didn't say one more word.

All the next day, Sunday, Dad hardly spoke. He just sat on the porch, staring out at the road, his eyes occasionally shifting back and forth rapidly, like he was seeing some kind of movie inside his head that nobody else could see. A few times, when Will came and leaned against him, Dad hugged him close or lay a hand on his head, whispered something to him, but that was the only sign Dad gave that he even knew anyone was there. And when we went to bed that night, I lay awake a long time, listening — listening.

Would he sneak out, go on to Dally's? Is this what he meant when he told Clara that he had found a "way," a way that worked for him?

But he didn't go. He didn't leave his room, and although I lay awake half the night listening, all I heard was the croak of the frogs and the mockingbird calling her lonesome nighttime song.

And then, next morning, Dad was still quiet when he got ready for work at the mill, and Will got quiet, too. Still, Dad went off to work, and us to school, and after school, Will and I carried on like things were the same. But I knew then I'd never see the ocean.

I guess it came as no surprise then that Dad didn't come home after work that day. We waited and waited, both of us looking out down the road, neither of us saying much. We started at about five, just when he should show up, and we kept it up, each of us sidling out to the porch every little while, like for air or something, pretending to the other that we weren't really looking. But when eight o'clock came and went, and the sun was beginning to slip behind the trees, and he still hadn't shown up, we sat down to eat.

I tried to be normal, pretend to Will that Dad was just delayed at work, but Will had gone as silent as Dad, so I had no idea if he believed me or not. Well, that's not the truth — I knew full well he didn't believe me. But what else could I do? Really, there wasn't anything else I could do.

Anyway, after supper, and after the washing up was done, I went and stood on the porch again, watching the night sky come down, looking from the road to the path through the field, then back again to the road to town.

But nobody or nothing moved along that road nor through the field. After a while, the sky went all dark, even the edges of the horizon losing the soft greenish glow, and the crickets and cicadas set up their evening song — and Dad still didn't come.

Will came out and stood beside me — he'd gone and taken a bath without being told — and his little body seemed extra small inside that big shirt of Dad's that he wore to bed. He just stood there with me, his hair wet, curling around his ears, looking out at the road, his eyes so wide and solemn-like, and then after a while, his hand sort of crept up and slid inside of mine.

We stood there for a long while, looking out, not speaking.

For some reason, though, standing there looking out on that empty road, I began to feel relieved.

Don't count on him, my voice had told me. *Don't count on him. Don't count on anything.*

But fool-like, I'd let myself be lulled. I'd let myself believe I'd take that trip, that I'd actually see the ocean. For those last weeks that he'd been coming and going as regular as the sun, somehow I'd begun to — well, maybe not exactly count on him, but hoped I could count on him, anyway. So it seemed a relief to stop. Nothing to disappoint you anymore.

"Come on, Will," I said finally, turning away from the road. "Bedtime."

He didn't argue, the way he argued every night that Dad was home, just came along with me, quiet-like.

I saw him to bed, tucked him in the way I'd been doing. Even when Dad was home, I tucked him in. It's our ritual. And after I have him tucked up tight, covers pulled in so snug he's like a baby in a papoose, then usually I sit and we read or talk some.

But this night, Will just turned his face to the wall before I had even finished tucking him, and his thumb crept into his mouth before I had turned out the light.

" 'Night, Gabby," he whispered.

I sat down on the bed. "Don't want to talk some?" I said.

"I'm sleepy," he said.

"Okay," I said. Because I really didn't feel like talking, either. " 'Night."

I got up, went to the door, turned, and looked back at him.

He lay there, still, very, very still.

"Will?" I said.

He didn't answer.

I went back and stood beside the bed. "Will," I said. "What are you doing?"

"Nothing," he said. But his voice was choked, trembly in his throat, and I knew just what he was doing — trying to hold back tears till I was out of the room. I'd seen him do it a zillion times before.

I sat down on the bed. "Will!" I said. "If you're going to cry, go ahead and cry."

"Huh? I'm sleeping," he whispered, but I could tell he was making his voice deliberately sleepy-sounding.

"You are not," I said. "Stop faking."

"I'm almost sleeping," he said.

"But you're not, I can tell," I said. "So, cry."

"No!" he said.

I sighed, stood up. "Okay," I said. "Fine."

I started out of the room again, but when I was right at the door, he spoke. "I don't cry anymore," he said.

"You don't?" I said.

"No," he said.

I came back and stood beside the bed again. "How come?" I said.

"How come, what?" he said.

"How come . . . you are so exasperating!" I said. "How come you don't cry anymore?"

"Because," he said.

"That's not an answer," I said. "You mean you don't cry ever? Not even when you're sad?"

"I'm not sad," he said.

"Liar," I said.

And this time, I did leave the room.

I went and sat on the porch, a feeling suddenly welling up inside of me, a feeling so big, so hurting, that I had to sit down. I realized I couldn't breathe, had to keep taking little tiny breaths, teeny, teeny ones, because there was no room for anything else inside me, no room for even air inside my chest. There was just this feeling. For a very long time I sat still, staring at the road, not moving, breathing shallow. I didn't feel mad. I didn't feel sad. I just felt — strange, a pain inside me, yet it wasn't a pain. Maybe it was just a hole. Yes, a hole, an empty place. I could put my hand right on where it was — in my middle, right below my chest, and I covered it with my hand.

I sat there thinking on that, when suddenly I saw a figure on the road — a man figure, someone carrying something slung over his shoulder, bent under the weight of it, just like that night Joseph had brought Dad home.

Joseph again? With Dad slung over his shoulder?

I jumped up, moved to the edge of the porch. I started to yell, don't bother, we don't want him back, dump him in town — but I stopped.

It wasn't Joseph.

And then I sucked in my breath because I could see exactly who it was. Dad. It was Dad. Dad, and he was whistling, one of those songs about dwarfs, and he was carrying this huge sack of something, bent under the weight of it.

He saw me standing there, nodded and grinned at me. "Pay day!" he called. "Wait till you see what I bought for you. Will, too. Where's Will?"

"In bed," I answered.

But of course Will wasn't in bed. He had appeared like a small shadow right beside me.

"Daddy?" he called.

He scurried down from the porch and hurried over to the road. "Can I help?" he said.

Dad shook his head. "Nope. If I put it down, I won't pick it up again. Just hold the door, and we'll see what we got here."

Will ran back to the porch and hurried to open the screen door, then held it wide, while Dad came in.

Dad dropped the huge sack on the floor by the table and sank into a chair.

He looked around.

"No supper?" he said.

"We already ate," I answered.

I made a point of looking at the wall clock. But at the same time, I felt guilty. He'd been in town, buying stuff for us. And we'd been blaming him.

"No matter, I guess," Dad said. "There's plenty in here."

And then he began emptying the sack, lifting out one thing after another, and laying it on the table. One after the other. Treasures, all kinds of treasures. For the house. For Will. For me.

__ Chapter 14 __

ONLY ONE THING WAS WRONG — the way Dad smelled. There was that smell on his breath, the smell of beer. Still, he didn't seem bad — I mean, not like drunk or anything, just smiling, cheerful, a lot more cheerful than he'd been the last few days. And anyway, I told myself, what was wrong with just having a beer or two? Dad was home. That's what was important. No sense fussing now. Not that I was fussing out loud or anything, just fussing inside my own head. And I had to make myself stop. Because maybe . . .

Anyway, I stood there, watching, smiling a little in spite of myself. Dad was emptying out this huge sack, and Will was helping him, reaching inside and pulling out each item like he was emptying an enormous Christmas stocking.

Dad had Will make three piles: one for Will, one for me, and one for the house.

"None for you, Daddy?" Will said.

"I don't need anything," Dad said. And he turned then and smiled at me, this sly grin on his face that got bigger and bigger. He even winked at me, like we had this big secret. "You wait," he said. "You just wait and see."

And then Dad put a couple things in my pile, things that were wrapped up in tissue paper and string, soft-looking, like they were — well, I wasn't even going to try and guess what they were.

I couldn't help getting a bit more excited then, pleased as punch, actually, especially about those things wrapped up in tissue.

And Will, he was just jiggling with excitement, shifting from one foot to the other, bouncing around like a dog with fleas. He kept climbing up onto a chair, standing on it to look down on all the stuff on the table, then sliding to the floor to pull another package out of the sack.

This went on for a long time, like it was a magic sack that might never be emptied, but of course it was. And then finally there was this huge pile of stuff there on the table, so much I could hardly believe it.

The pile for the house was big — but my pile was even bigger. And most of mine was wrapped up so I couldn't see what was hiding inside.

In the house pile there was a canned ham, a package of

bacon, sugar and potatoes and eggs and peanut butter and coffee and tuna — boring stuff, all of it, but important, basic stuff, stuff to get you through the ordinary times, and through the bad times, too. And there were other things, too, things I'd never seen in my whole entire life, and wouldn't have bought, either, not if I'd been with him when he shopped, yet I couldn't wait to try some of them. There were canned artichokes, and canned sausage, and snails — again, he had bought snails! But what difference? He wanted them, I guess. There was canned spaghetti, and packages of prunes and dried apricots, and even cookies, chocolate sandwich cookies. There was apple butter, and regular butter, and pork rinds and pickles and — Lord, I couldn't even say what-all.

I looked over at Will's pile. There were two or three things wrapped in that tissue paper, but most of the rest were just piled there, and I could see them all. There were clothes, pants and shirts, and a pair of slippers, slippers! Will had never had slippers. Well, I hadn't, either, but I didn't care. But Will, he was so excited, he grabbed the slippers, put them on, soft moccasins like, beaded around the front, like Indian shoes, and with little bits of fur on the sides.

"Look, Gabby!" Will said, leaning back in his chair and sticking his legs out in front so I could see. "Look at them."

I nodded. "I see," I said. "They're beautiful."

"I look just like an Indian brave, right?" he said.

"Right," Dad said. "And you are brave."

Will looked at Dad, smiled.

Dad nodded. "Know how many times I've told you that? You're brave, very, very brave."

Will just shrugged, then looked at me. "You open something," he said.

I looked at my pile, picked up one small package, and felt it gently.

Soft. It was soft, like maybe it was a dress or a skirt or something. But then I shook my head and put the package down. For some reason, I was uneasy — would rather wait, would rather wonder than see it right now.

"Show me something else, Will," I said.

Will happily reached into his pile, picked up a folded piece of clothing — a shirt? — and frowned down at it. He turned it over and over in his hands, a puzzled look on his face, and then suddenly he began to smile.

He looked up at me, wide-eyed. "Look, Gabby!" he said, his voice just above a whisper. "Look."

He shook out the shirt and held it up to himself — only it wasn't any ordinary shirt. It was a pajama shirt, and there were pajama bottoms, too.

Will had never had pajamas.

These were red, with little black-and-white dogs scattered all over them — those spotty dalmatians dogs, like firemen have — at least they're supposed to have, but I have never seen one in real life, not even when I was in kindergarten, and the firemen used to come to talk to us about fire safety.

Will jumped up, yanked off the shirt he was wearing, and pulled the top over him, his little head appearing out of the opening, grinning at Dad and me.

"Look at me!" he said, and then he pulled on the bottom part, too, and he turned around so we could admire him, around and around.

The pajamas were big for him, the top as long as a dress, the bottoms dragging on the floor, covering up his new moccasin slippers. But they weren't way too big, more like they would fit him in a year or so.

I looked over at Dad. He did have some good sense.

Dad was smiling at me. "Come on, Gabby," he said. "Your turn."

I took a deep breath, then picked up one of the packages and felt it.

"This one?" I said.

Dad nodded. "Any one," he said.

I bit my lip and bent over the package. I didn't know what I wanted to find in there. New jeans? The kind Mallie'd gotten the other day?

But no, the package was too small for jeans.

I was excited, and sort of strange-feeling, too — nervous, maybe. Why? It wasn't that I needed anything really, even wanted anything especially, although new jeans would be nice.

"Go on!" Dad said. "Go on. We want to see."

I looked at him, then at Will.

Will was bouncing up and down on his chair, his little face all damp and sweaty from excitement.

"Hurry, Gabby!" he said. "We want to see."

Slowly, my fingers shaking a little — dumb me — I undid the string, folded back the edges of the paper, and fingered what was inside.

What was it?

I looked up at Dad, but he just shrugged and smiled at me.

I bent over the package again and tore back more of the paper.

Whatever it was, it was soft, and the most beautiful color, green, a sort of blue-green, like winter wheat just coming ripe. But it was slippery feeling, too, kind of rubbery-like. What was it?

I tore back the rest of the paper, then lifted it out and held it up.

It was . . . it was a . . .

I looked at Dad, my eyes suddenly filling with tears.

"Oh, Dad!" I whispered, and I hugged it close it to me.

A bathing suit, it was a bathing suit, a bathing suit!

"For your trip to the ocean," Dad said.

Tears began streaming down my cheeks, just pouring down.

"Oh, Gabrielle," Dad said. "What's wrong? Don't you like it? I can take it back. I'll get you a different color. I'll get a different —"

"No!" I said. "No, don't take it back. It's — it's just beautiful."

"Try it on!" Will said. "Gabby, go try it on. Oh, why are you crying?"

I shook my head "I'm not crying," I said. "I'm not. I'm just . . ."

But the tears were running down my face.

"I'll go try it on," I said.

I fled to my room, slammed the door, and leaned back against it. I wasn't just crying. I was sobbing. But then I just bent over, slipped out of my clothes, and stepped into the suit.

It was hard to wriggle into — I'd never had a bathing suit before, never put one on.

I had to yank and tug and pull at it, edging it up over my thighs, my hips, trying to wipe away tears at the same time, but finally I had wiggled into it, pulled it up, fitted the straps over my shoulders — and looked at myself in the mirror.

It fit. That's the first thing I noticed, fit like I had picked it out for myself, tried it on in the store. And the second thing I thought was, I looked — well — I sort of looked — I mean, I did, I looked good! It looked nice on me, fit in the right places.

I tugged it, smoothed it down a bit.

A bathing suit.

I stood in front of the mirror, turned this way, that, my mind racing, thinking thoughts, then turning back on itself and thinking different thoughts. Me. I was standing there wearing a bathing suit.

A bathing suit so I could go to the ocean.

Dad was telling me he planned to stay. He was promising to stay, that's what this meant, promising to stay and to be good. Sober. He was telling me I could count on him. I could go and he would stay. And Will wouldn't be left alone.

Fool, my voice whispered.

I took a deep breath and held it, didn't move at all for a moment. Maybe if I didn't answer, didn't even blink, maybe she'd go away.

You're being a fool, the voice whispered again.

I let out my breath, leaned closer to the mirror, and looked hard at myself. *He spent his money on us,* I whispered back silently. *He spent it on food, on the things we need. On a bathing suit. It's a promise. And he came home.*

He smells, doesn't he? the voice said. *His breath stinks.*

"So what?!" I said, angry, furious, my voice rising — and for the first time ever, I realized I had answered it out loud. I stood very still then, my heart pounding, head tilted to the door, wondering if Dad or Will had heard. But they were laughing together, and I heard Will suddenly squeal, probably had just opened a package or tried on something.

I turned back, put my hand to my throat, felt my heart beating hard there. *Stop it!* I whispered — silently again. *He's . . . he's different now.*

Ha! the voice said.

You wait and see, I said. *Just wait and see.*

No answer.

I said, *Just give it a chance, wait and see. That's sensible, fair, isn't it, to wait and see what happens?*

But still there was no answer.

So I whispered once more, *Just wait and see what happens.*

⸺ Chapter 15 ⸺

SCHOOL CLOSED, and in just one more week we'd go to the ocean. And I was going! I'd made up my mind. Dad had promised. He'd proved he could be counted on. Well — at least this time. He went to work each day. He came home each night. He didn't slip off during the night to Dally's. And more than anything, he'd bought me the bathing suit. It was like a promise, better than a promise, really. It was proof that he intended to stay with Will. So I could go.

I'd never been so excited.

Those next days were the most delicious, dreamy, exciting days of my whole, entire life. I began to realize then why Mallie talks the way she does — all those fancy words, all those extra-excited kinds of words. She talks like that because she feels like that, filled up with excitement, filled up with all that stuff inside, so much so that it just bursts out of her in fancy, sparkling words. I even began to feel bad about how much I teased her, when I'd tell her she talks too much, because I realized that she talks like that because she *has* to, because the words just burst out of her.

They were bursting out of me, too. I was so filled up with words, with happiness, that they spilled out into my notebook — I filled an entire notebook in just one week — and then they even spilled out into songs. I found myself singing little snatches of songs like those old Billy Joel songs that Mom used to sing: Uptown girl, you've been living in an uptown world . . .

I even wished I were a bird — well, maybe I didn't exactly want to *be* a bird, because I remembered what Mallie said that day when we saw the bird of God and she said how birds got mites or fleas or something. I didn't want fleas or mites, but if I was that bird, I'd sing. Boy, would I sing. I would sing.

Only thing was Will. We'd never been apart, not ever. But Dad said not to worry. He said there was a lady who provided day care for people who worked at the mill, and Will could go there in the daytime. Best of all, it was someone Will knew, this lady named Sparkle — that's her full name, first and last, just plain Sparkle. Sparkle cleans the church and changes the flowers and plays the organ, and even teaches the Sunday school kids, the little ones. Will had been in her Sunday school class for three years, and he liked her. She'd just started this day care. Only problem was, it cost money. But Dad said not to worry about that, either.

I was so happy. I was just so happy.

If Dad just stayed okay.

He would stay okay.

My voice had left me — can't say I was sorry to see it go — but I did wonder what it would say now. I mean, seeing me so happy, so fixed on going. I wondered if it would call me a fool.

But never mind. Each day, when Dad got home — and he did come home each and every day almost on time — we talked about all the things I would see and do on the trip. Dad wanted me to remember every single thing, wanted me to write it all down and tell him when I got back.

New notebooks — that's what had been inside one of my paper packages — and I didn't even know that Dad knew I kept notebooks. But I set one aside — it had a blue-green cover, just like my bathing suit — and that would be my notebook about the ocean. And then I set another one aside, a red one, and that would be the one for private thoughts, ones I didn't want to share with anybody, my autobiography book.

I was counting the days, actually marking them off on my calendar. Mallie's mother, she wanted to know if she should come over and talk to Dad before we left, tell him where we'd be and what kinds of things I'd need to bring, but I told her no. Dad is shy with people, almost as shy as Will, even with neighbors like them, who we'd known for years. So I just told her to make a list of what Dad should know — places we'd be, stuff I needed — and give it to me to give to Dad.

Only thing on the list that I didn't have was rain gear, because in my packages were a lot of clothes, jeans even, and new shorts and a sweatshirt. And when I told Dad about the raincoat, he right away stopped at the store in town and bought me one — a bright yellow slicker that came all the way down to my feet, with a hooded thing for my head, silliest thing I'd ever seen. I looked like one of those pictures of fishermen that you see in the backs of magazines, advertising throat drops or cough drops or something. But it sure would keep me dry, and it might come in handy someday, never could tell.

Funny thing was, though, Will had gotten quiet again. Dad was home, was talking to Will and playing with him, but Will had that look he got when Dad was gone. He'd even stopped arguing with me, began doing what I told him to do. And that wasn't normal at all. Was it my going that was worrying him? Or something else?

Well, he'd get over it, whatever it was.

One night, though, when the three of us were having dinner, I looked over at Will. He had been playing with his food, frowning down at his plate, pushing his biscuits from one side of the plate to another. I had made those biscuits specially for him that day — knew he loved them, thought maybe it would perk him up. And here I'd baked them up and buttered them, and he wouldn't even touch them.

"What's the matter with you?" I said.

He didn't look up. "Nothing," he said.

"Is, too," I said.

"Is not!" he said, making a frowning face at his plate.

"Ha!" I said. And I thought how much I sounded like that voice that used to come argue with me.

"Well, it's not," he said. He looked up at Dad. "I'm all right — right, Daddy?" he said.

Dad tilted his head to one side. "I don't know," he said. "Seems to me you've been a bit winchy lately."

"What?" Will said.

Dad laughed. "Winchy. It means . . . I'm not sure what it means, but when I was your age, that's what Clara said about me. It meant to me anything that wasn't — well, wasn't quite right."

"Oh," Will said.

"There!" I said. "Dad thinks so, too. So how come?"

Will just shrugged, then looked down at his plate again and began breaking up his biscuits into little bitty pieces.

I just shook my head. Then I got up, went to the stove, and brought back the bean pot to ladle out seconds. Dad loves beans, and I'd made not just the biscuits but a great big pot of beans with salt pork and bacon, the stuff Dad had brought home that night.

I put a spoonful onto Dad's plate, another onto mine. Will hadn't eaten a thing, so there was no sense putting anything more on his plate.

"And besides," I said, "you haven't touched your biscuits."

"I'm cutting them up," Will said.

I sighed, put the pot back on the stove, and sat back down. Dad and I went about eating. And Will went about pushing his food around. I didn't try again. Knowing Will, he'd talk when he felt like talking. If at all.

We were all through eating — Dad and me, anyway — and I had just begun to clear the table, when Will spoke. "Sparkle," he said.

"Sparkle, what?" I said.

"I don't want to go there," he said.

"You don't want to go to Sparkle's?" I said. "How come?"

He shrugged.

I looked at Dad. He was looking at Will, puzzled-like.

"Why not, son?" Dad said.

"Because."

"But you like Sparkle," I said.

"I know," Will said.

"So?" I said.

"So I don't want to go there." He looked up at Dad. "Could Clara come instead?" he said hopefully.

"Oh, I don't know about that!" Dad said quickly. "I don't think so."

"Why not?" Will said.

Dad just shook his head, didn't answer.

"What's wrong with Sparkle?" I said.

"Nothing!" Will said. "I told you."

He made a face at me, crossing his eyes, then sticking out his tongue.

I suddenly laughed, couldn't help it — the first sign of life I'd seen from him in days.

"Stop laughing!" he said. And he burst out crying.

He put his head on the table, one hand curled over the back of his neck, the way he does, like he's protecting that scar. And he cried.

For a minute, I just stared at him. Dad did, too.

Then Dad got up, went to Will's chair, and lifted Will up into his arms. Then he carried Will back to his own place and sat down, snuggling Will into his lap.

"It's okay," Dad crooned, rocking Will back and forth, back and forth. "It's okay."

Will just cried. And cried. And I felt terrible sad. I hadn't meant to make him cry, not at all.

"I'm sorry, Will," I said. "I wasn't laughing at you."

"Were, too," he sobbed, and wiped his nose on his sleeve.

I started to say, don't do that! — but I clamped my mouth shut.

There was a long silence, and then Will whispered, "Dogs."

"Dogs?" Dad said.

"Sparkle has dogs," Will said.

"Oh," Dad said.

"Oh, boy," I said. "Oh, boy."

I went around the table, crouched down beside Will, and reached for his hand. He didn't let me take it, hugged himself closer to Dad.

"Will," I said, "maybe she can keep them caged up or something. How many does she have?"

"One," Will said. "She just got it. A big one!"

"How big?" I said.

Will sat up straight, put out his hands, measuring a space in the air, his hands just about a foot apart.

"That's little," I said. "Is it a puppy?"

"It's a dog!" Will said, and he buried his face against Dad again.

"Tell you what, Will," Dad said. "I have an idea. How about I take that dog to work with me? Or make sure it's in a pen somewhere. I'll figure it out. I'll make sure it's not there when you're there, how's that?"

"That's a great idea," I said.

But Will didn't answer, just leaned closer against Dad. And then — what was with him? — he began to cry even harder. Yet Dad had just said he'd take care of it! Honestly, if Will caused some ruckus, kept me from going, I'd . . . I didn't know what I'd do.

I looked at Dad, and he just shrugged. But he hugged

Will close, rocking him some more. "What is it?" Dad whispered. "Come on, Will boy, can't you tell me? You're a brave boy, you can say it."

"But I'm not brave!" Will said, and he practically wailed it. "I'm not brave at all."

"Oh, Will!" Dad said. "You are brave. You're the bravest boy of all."

"I'm not," Will sobbed. "I'm scared of dogs."

"Oh," Dad said, rocking Will, rocking him, rocking him. "Oh."

"I'm a scared cat," Will sobbed.

"Oh," Dad said again. "That's it? That you're scared?"

"Yes!" Will said. Well, actually, he yelled it.

"Will?" Dad said. "Now, hush, boy. Will, don't you know most everybody's scared of something? That's nothing to be shamed about."

"You're not scared!" Will said. "Gabby's not scared."

"I am too scared," I said. "Lots of times, I am. Dogs, no, but other stuff."

Will peeked out at me from Dad's arms. "What?" he said.

I looked at him, then at Dad. I shrugged. "Lots of things," I said.

Will just frowned at me, his lower lip jutted out.

And then, like I had to prove it to him, I blurted out, "Like the full moon!" I said. "I'm scared sometimes that the moon brings bad things out — I mean, not just owls and coyotes — but really bad things, ghosts and were-wolves!"

Will scrunched up his face at me. "There's no such thing as ghosts or werewolves," he said.

"I know that!" I said, and my voice came out meaner, more angry than I meant it to, because I felt the fool for blurting that out, and I could feel my face flush hot. But I was also relieved that I hadn't been dumb enough to blurt out the bigger worries, the real ones — that Dad would go off again, that you couldn't count on him, that there was a voice that kept badgering me, and most of the time it was right, and whose voice was it, anyway? Ghosts and werewolves were just little worries, compared to the others.

Will looked up at Dad then. "But you don't get scared, right, Daddy?" he said, his voice all quavery-like. "Right?"

It was odd the way Will said it, the way he looked at Dad — tentative, hopeful? Like he wanted Dad not to be scared — but maybe wanted to know he was, too?

And Dad, I didn't know what he was thinking, if he knew what Will wanted or not. All I know is that Dad nodded; several times he nodded. And then he suddenly hugged Will close, bent his head over him, hugged him so close that I heard Will's breath puff out of him, hard, fast, like he'd been squeezed too hard.

Dad kept his head against Will's like that for a long,

long time, just holding him close, and nobody said anything. And then, after a bit, Dad spoke. "Will," he whispered, "this old man...oh, your daddy has fears, demons, every bit as bad as dogs, son — oh, bad as dogs."

Will took a deep breath, nodded. And then, just like that, he slid out of Dad's lap. He wiped his eyes and his nose in his shirt, then scooted back to his place, sat down and picked up his fork.

He looked up at me, smiled a little, though his face was still all streaky with tears. "I like fiddleheads," he said.

I just rolled my eyes, put my hands on my hips. "I know that!" I said. "Why else do you think I made them?"

Chapter 16

FIRST THING I THOUGHT NEXT AFTERNOON, late, when Will and I came out of the woods after picking up more sticks for his figures, was that Will's wish had been granted, that Clara had come. But that made no sense at all, because why would she come now? Yet there was that lemon-yellow pickup truck of hers in front of our house, and someone — someone big — was sitting on the porch steps.

There were other people there, too, and a car parked behind the pickup truck. Even from the meadow's edge, I could see that the car was kind of official-looking, had seals on the side, like county cars, like that social worker car and —

We stopped, and I looked at Will and he at me. His hand slid into mine.

"G-Gabby?" he said.

"Hush," I said.

I held tight to his hand, held him there, looked some more. No sense rushing out there, till we could tell what was what.

"Who are they?" Will whispered.

I shrugged. "Don't know," I said.

"Where's Dad?" Will said.

"At work, of course!" I said, and I knew my voice was snappy, but he was such a baby sometimes.

"Is that Clara?" Will said, leaning forward, squinting against the sun, and his voice was suddenly brighter, hopeful.

"Looks like it," I said.

"Goody!" Will said, and he pulled his hand out of mine, and before I could stop him, he took off, running, running toward Clara.

I watched him go, didn't move, just stood watching, looking at them all gathered there, looking at the county car, looking at Clara who'd come to us just once before — just that once — watching Will speed toward them. Watching and thinking, thinking that this was one of those times when the whole world would change. Things were one way now, and once I got to that porch, they'd never be the same again. Don't ask how I knew those things, but I did. Didn't take any great brains. All you had to do was look and see.

Will ran across the meadow to Clara, ran through flowers, Indian paint brush flowers high as his head, calling, "Clara! Clara!" and I saw her turn to him, saw that she spied me standing back by the woods, raised a hand to me.

Still, I didn't move to go to them, just stood, watched, holding on to now. But after a minute, I found myself going up there, too, walking, walking, one foot in front of the other, my feet taking me. One foot, another, heavy old feet, right up to the steps.

And then I was there, at the porch, and there was Will, setting up right close to Clara on the step, and Clara, she had an arm around him, had him hugged close, and nobody was saying anything. Not a single word.

On the edge of the porch was the sheriff, dressed up in his fancy uniform, creases down the legs and even down the back of his shirt. He was holding his hat in his hands, and he had those glinty sunglasses on so I couldn't see his eyes, and he didn't say anything, either. Mallie's mother was there, too — Mallie's mother! She was all red-eyed, scared-looking almost, and when I came up on the porch, she reached a hand out toward me, fingers spread. But then she dropped her hand to her side, shook her head.

And then Clara looked up at them and said, "You all go on home now. I'll take care of this."

They did, left, like they were plenty glad to go, practically running, the sheriff did, anyway. Mallie's mama, she bent and whispered something to Clara, then she just sighed big, shook her head again, and then she scuttled away, too.

When they were all gone, Clara, she reached a hand out to me, like to gather me in, just like she was gathering in Will, but I stayed where I was, right by the railing.

"What?" I said.

She looked away from me and down at Will, and I looked at Will, too. He was huddled close to her, hugging himself to himself, and I could see he was shivering, even though the sun was shining hot.

Clara moved him in closer, looked up at me then, her eyes wide and clear, but with dark inside them, dark pools of something. While I waited on her words.

"Your daddy," Clara said, her voice quiet, calm like the wind. "He's dead. There was an accident at the mill."

Right away, Will began to wail, just wail, like one of those puppy dogs he hates so, just wailed and wailed, howled practically. And Clara, she gathered him closer in those big, wide arms, smothering him practically, looked like from here.

Me, I didn't move, stayed still as a stick. Thought nothing either, nothing. Wasn't even there anymore, felt like that anyway, wasn't even there, like I had gone away from myself. I could even see me, looking down on myself, like there was a me here on this porch, and then a space above my head, and on top of that space, I was up there, looking down at me.

Not feeling anything.

But my voice came back, the way it does sometimes, especially when I don't want it.

Told you, it said. *Told you not to count on him.*

_ Chapter 17 _

THE DAYS THAT FOLLOWED were all like that for me—
quiet, not there, just looking down on all this mess, stay-
ing still, silent.

Will, though, he made enough noise for both of us,
carried on something fierce, especially when we went to
the funeral place where Dad was, what was left of him
anyway, his dead body, one leg practically cut all the way
off from that mill saw, though they had fixed him up
good so you couldn't see that. Will and I stood beside
that wooden box they'd put him in, stood looking down
on his old, tired face, and Will, well, I thought he'd never
stop his bawling, cried so hard he began to hiccup. He
kept rocking, hugging himself to himself, though every
little while, he'd reach for my hand, but I shook him off,

didn't want to touch him, didn't want to touch anybody. So then he went to Clara to cry.

Me, I didn't cry, not at all. Not at all. Felt nothing, either, nothing. Once, silly, but I checked on my heartbeat, held my fingers on my wrist, to see was my heart beating, was I breathing? That part, the breathing part, that seemed to come hard. I felt like my breath had gone away from me, that way you get when you run hard. I kept trying for air, taking bigger and bigger breaths, looking to get enough air inside, couldn't get enough.

But I was alive all right. Breathing. Thinking. Thinking how I sure couldn't have seen this particular thing coming our way, him leaving us like this. But why not? It was the kind of stupid thing he'd do.

And yet . . . and yet, I didn't really believe it, believe he was gone for good, I mean. No, no, that's not the truth, I did believe it, but I didn't believe it, too. Both of those things were true.

Even when we sat around the funeral place — having a wake is what they called it — I had that funny way of feeling. Maybe it was my voice. Maybe she believed and I didn't believe, or the other way round. Anyway, he'd left so many other times, who was to say he wouldn't come back again? I couldn't figure it, didn't try. It was just too much for my head right then.

Not many people came to that wake, seeing as how

Dad didn't have many friends. Of course, Joseph came and his wife, Francie, too, but not many other people at all. Not that it mattered much. Dad was in that box. That's what mattered.

Then one more day and it was funeral day, day to put him away for good. I was out standing on the porch, showered and dressed, waiting, and Clara, she was inside in the house with Will, and we were going to go to the churchyard in her truck to meet Dad and say prayers over him and bury him there, right next to Mom. No more waiting for him, no more worrying, no more nothing. A relief, that's what it was.

After a bit, Clara came out with Will, and Will, he wasn't sobbing his head off for a change, and the three of us climbed in Clara's truck, and off we went.

Will, he didn't reach for my hand, but he kept looking at me, kind of sideways-like, but I pretended not to see.

After a while, though, he whispered, "Gabby?"

"What?" I said.

He didn't answer.

"What?" I said again, my voice coming out hard-like.

"Nothing," he whispered.

I just shook my head. Hate it when he does that, just hate it.

And then we were there, and the pastor was already waiting for us, standing there in the sun, a prayer book in his hand. He was wearing his long black robe that came all the way down to the ground, and there was this ribbon thing hanging round his neck. It made me think of a girl who had been just about to tie up her hair, but then forgot and left the ribbon dangling over her shoulders, and I couldn't help wondering why ministers dressed like women for funerals and stuff.

The funeral men were there, too, with Dad's casket, and over the casket and the open grave, they had set up this awning thing, like to keep the sun off. But why would you want to keep the sun off him, when it was the last time he'd ever be in the sun?

Clara went up to speak to the funeral men, and Will, he sidled up to me, right close to me, looked up at me, not saying anything, just looking, that wide-eyed look.

"What?" I said.

"Nothing," he whispered. But he kept looking at me, and then his hand slid up, reached for my hand.

I just rolled my eyes at him, took a deep breath. "Okay," I said. And I let his hand come into mine.

We both looked over the churchyard then, looked toward the casket, top all nailed down and shiny-like, a wreath of limp pink roses lying on top, the ribbon saying, *From your beloved children,* but this beloved child had had nothing to do with it.

"Now that we're all here, shall we begin?" Pastor

Richards said, looking at Will and me, like we had a choice, right?

Then, without waiting for an answer, Pastor Richards began, and Will leaned into me, and it was all a mistake. That's what I was thinking: everything was a mistake, all of life was a mistake. It was especially a mistake to let Will hold my hand. His was all warm and wet and trembly, and after a minute, I could feel something in my throat, and I let go of Will's hand, bent to tie my shoe, and when I stood up, I folded my hands tight in front of me.

Pastor Richards didn't say anything new, just all the usual stuff you'd expect a pastor to say, how God was waiting for our father right this minute, how Dad had no more worries and was at peace, held safe in the Lord's arms, and I just shook my head, wondering how Dad felt about that, being in anybody's arms, especially the Lord's, wondered, too, how the Lord felt about that. And I couldn't help wondering how was it fair or not fair, how Dad should have no more worries, when we were left with so many. And then Pastor Richards said about suffer all the little children to come unto Him, that the Lord would give us peace. And I couldn't help thinking, ha!

And then, that was that.

Pastor Richards asked if Will or I wanted to put the first shovelful of earth on Dad, and I shook my head, but

Will went up, snuffling, wiping his nose on his shirt, and I noticed he had something in his hand, something that looked like a stick man, couldn't even one day leave his dumb old stick men at home. And then he dropped his little stick man down on the casket, down into that hole.

I turned away. Stupid, that's what it was. Stupid, all of this.

And then I heard a sound, a clunk kind of sound, like Will had dropped the earth down on him, and I couldn't wait to be out of there, and I went to the truck all by myself, waited for them there.

And then it was over. And we were home.

I went right to my room, changed out of my skirt — hadn't worn the new one Dad had bought, had just worn the old one — and into my regular clothes, and I went to the kitchen where Will and Clara had set themselves down, eating some popcorn Clara had made, both of them, like it was Saturday afternoon at the movies or something.

I looked up at the clock, twelve o'clock, went over to the refrigerator, started looking for something to make.

Casseroles. There were four or five in there that people from the church had brought. I took one out, didn't matter what, slid it into the oven, turned the oven on.

I looked at Clara then. "You can go home now," I said. "We can manage."

She shook her head. "I don't think so," she said.

"I think so," I said.

She raised her eyebrows at me. "Why don't I just wait awhile?" she said.

"For what?" I said. "He's not coming back."

She didn't answer, but Will, he began to snuffle again.

I glared at him, and he quick looked down, took a big, trembly breath, seemed to hold it in.

Good. I was tired of his snuffles.

"Why don't you sit awhile?" Clara said to me, pulling out a chair and patting it.

"Sit?" I said. "There's work to do."

"Work can wait," Clara said. "It always does."

"Not around here," I said. I wanted to add, we're not dirty like in your house, but I didn't, didn't say any of the mean things that were suddenly wanting to burst out of me — like what are you hanging around for, what did you come for in the first place, who invited you, told you about Dad, even? Things I'd thought about, but why bother?

I left her and Will there, scooping up their handfuls of popcorn, and went outside to the porch, stood there looking over the fields, wondering, wondering. I'd seen him in the box, seen him, knew it was him. Still, I couldn't figure it. I mean, he'd just been there, hugging up Will, telling us about fears. "Oh, your daddy has fears, demons, every bit as bad as dogs," he'd said.

And was he afraid when that mill saw ripped through his leg, was he?

And then, there was Mallie coming across the road. She had another casserole in her hands, one her mama had cooked up for us probably.

Mallie, she looked scared, and she didn't say anything to me when she stepped up on that porch, just held out the dish, and I took it, and I didn't say anything back to her, either. So for a long time we just stood there, looking at each other. I wondered then if maybe she knew I wasn't really there, so why bother with talking?

But she stood there such a long time, just looking at me, that finally I said, "What?"

"We put off our trip," she said, her voice just above a whisper. "We're going to wait an extra week before we go."

I squinted up my eyes at her. "What for?" I said.

"For you," she said. "My mom said to give you a chance to feel better. Or . . . I don't know. But she said it would help if we waited some."

I shook my head. "Don't bother," I said.

"But we already did," she said. "My dad had reservations at campgrounds and stuff, but he changed them all." She looked out at the fields, blinking hard a minute, then back at me, and her eyes were shiny. "Gabby?" she said. "Gabby?"

"Tell your mother thanks for the dish," I said. I turned

and started into the house. But then I stopped, took a breath, didn't turn round to face her, though. "Tell her," I said, "tell her to just go on with your vacation, don't wait for me. I've changed my mind."

"Changed your mind?" Mallie said.

"Yeah, changed my mind," I said. "I don't want to see the ocean after all."

__Chapter 18__

NEXT DAY, I tried to get rid of Clara again, but she just said, "Not yet, girl," and she kept sitting there at that table, talking to Will, letting him cry himself out in her arms. She kept her eyes fixed hard on me, though, every time I came into that room, eyebrows raised up till they practically met her hairline, like she expected me to say something, but whatever it was she expected, I wasn't giving it. She didn't do many other things, though, and that was good, letting me do all the meals and such, same as always. Not that it mattered much, wasn't much different, seeing as how there were three of us before and three of us now, so meals weren't any trouble.

Once in a while, I wondered what we would do about money and all, Will and me, with Dad gone again, but it didn't trouble me much, don't know why. Actually I didn't worry much about anything, still didn't feel anything. Funny. Nothing. Even my voice seemed to know I wasn't there, had gone clear away.

Had to do something, though, so what I did was walk. I just walked, that day, next day, next, walked and walked. And I mean, really walked. I walked the fields, walked to town, went to church, though I didn't go in, just walked around, looked at stuff, peered over the fence into the graveyard, but didn't go in. No need to do that. I even peered in the windows of the school some days.

Then each day, when it got to be suppertime, I went home and made up supper, and later, when it got really late, when the stars began to fill up the sky and the moon was big, ready to light my way, then I got up and walked some more.

I snuck out quietly, didn't want to wake Will nor Clara, walked myself to town, just watching people come and go, not that there were many, except by the bars. But then one night, I found myself outside one of the bars, the one Dad hung around in. Well, he hung in all of them, but specially Dally's, and I made my way in there.

I went real cautious-like, kept my eyes open for that awful Harry, wouldn't let myself get caught up in his wretched arms again.

I made my way past the bar, through the crowd, moving slowly, looking round me. Funny, nobody seemed to notice me. I wondered then if it had happened, if I'd gotten to be real invisible, really not there, not anywhere. And wouldn't that be something, if I was just like Dad, not anywhere anymore? But then I saw someone, and he saw me, I could tell he saw me, and at first — don't know why — my heart did this thing in my chest, like I was glad to see him, but probably not, probably not.

"Gal!" Joseph said. "What are you doing here?"

I just shook my head.

He took my arm, led me to a bench, sat me down. "What are you here for?" he said. "You belong in bed this time of night."

I didn't answer, just shrugged.

Joseph looked me over real good, like that doctor did to Will that time, squinty-eyed, like he was trying to figure out what's inside you even before he looks down your throat and into your ears.

"You're hurting, Gal," Joseph said, and his voice was calm and still as water.

I shook my head no.

"You surely are," he said softly. "But this is no place to make it better, Gal, no place at all."

"I'm okay," I said.

"You don't belong here," he said.

I shrugged. "It's okay," I said again.

"Not okay," he said. He let his eyes sweep round the place, over at the men milling at the bar, at the ones around the dart game, yelling and hooting and swearing.

"And you're going to be a lot less okay if you stay around here," he added.

"Won't stay long," I said. "Just looking for something." And I realized suddenly that was the truth. God above, I had said the truth. Because this was the place.

Joseph squinted up his eyes at me. "What do you mean?" he said. "Looking for what?"

I shrugged, shook my head, hadn't meant to let that much out. Hadn't thought that much, actually. Just blurted out the words, and just like that, the thought had come with them. Because if there was anyplace he'd be, this was the place.

Joseph lowered his head, his chin so low it was almost resting on his chest, and he stayed that way awhile. After a bit, he looked up at me. "For your daddy?" he said quietly. "That who you're looking for?"

No answer, how to answer? I just closed my eyes, felt my heart pounding hard, fearsome, waiting, waiting for him to say it, to tell me that bad thing, he was going to tell me . . . that Dad . . . no.

I opened my eyes, stared down at my hands. Take a breath, I told myself, take a breath, in, out, keep taking breaths. I kept working on that a long time, staring at my hands, making breaths come in, out, shaky, though, and Joseph, all that time, he didn't say a single word.

After a bit, I began working my hands, twisting them round and round each other, tight, one holding on the other. Then I took another breath, swallowed, and I looked up at Joseph, and a voice — me? — said that stupid thing, that really, really stupid thing. "You'll bring him home if he shows up?" I said.

Joseph looked back at me, and his eyes, they were so black I could see myself in there, really see me looking back at me, and I thought, how come I was in there?

"You will?" I said.

Joseph nodded. "I will," he answered. "I'll bring him home. If he shows up."

I closed my eyes, felt my breath move easy then, in, out, easy like, real easy.

Joseph put a hand on my elbow. "But now, Gabby," he said, "now I'm going to walk you home."

I opened my eyes, swallowed hard, tried to swallow, but a lump had suddenly come up, was coming up, something was, and it was hot, and it tasted bad, sour, burning, and it welled up in my throat. Something else welled up, too, something hot, wet, swimming up into my eyes.

I shook my head, shook off his hand. "No need," I said. "I'll go."

"I'll go along with you," a voice said, a voice right there at my elbow, and I looked up and there was Clara, Clara right there, looking down at me, and her eyes were extra-shiny.

I frowned at her. "What are you doing here?" I said.

She didn't answer, just moved her huge shoulders up, then down.

"You're supposed to be with Will!" I said, angry-like, and I knew it was dumb. Nobody had asked her to care for Will. What was I expecting of her, anyway?

But she had moved herself in, so the least she could do was be responsible. I just shook my head. But it figured.

I stood up, turned to Joseph.

He had put a hand on Clara's arm, and the two of them were looking at me sad-like, like I was . . . like they were . . . like they knew something. Like they knew it, too. About Dad not showing up, not ever anymore.

"Don't," I said, and I put up a hand, like to stop something, but I didn't know what, just didn't know.

I just knew I had to go. Get away. And I did.

Chapter 19

Run, that's what I had to do. Run. Run. All through the fields, all the way, had to get away, run fast, run. But where, where, where to go? When I was small, there were times I'd hide in my closet or under my bed. But I didn't want to be in that house, not near where he'd been, but he'd been everywhere, maybe still was everywhere, even though he was nowhere anymore. Never would be.

Under the porch, that was a place — used to play there when I was small, when I was small, and Lord, once I lit matches under there, nearly set the house on fire.

There was a crawl place under there, and a door. I could go there. I wasn't too big for it even now — I wasn't. And then what, what?

No, no — night creatures down there, night things,

ghosts and werewolves. Of course there aren't any of those things, but Lord, were there?

I slowed, slowed my running, just a bit, looked behind, not for haunts or werewolves, for Clara. Was she coming on? Didn't want to see her.

But there was no sign of her, just the moon shining bright, bright like it was day almost, and I thought of Mom and how she used to sing in the moonlight, and then — Lord, Mom! She was gone, dead and gone, and Dad, were she and Dad together now? And was that fair? Them up there, us left here?

And Dad had promised, he had. He'd bought the bathing suit, his promise.

I stopped then, stock-still, right there in that meadow, thinking about that. That was a thing I could do, a real thing, could do it now. But I'd have to go in there, in that house where he used to be — didn't know why that bothered me now, hadn't before, but Lord, wasn't everything different now, wasn't it?

I began running again, made it home, not even pausing to breathe, and then to my room, hoped Will was sleeping, and found that knapsack, packed, packed for Mom's ocean, where I wasn't going anymore.

I grabbed up the pack, dug through, felt the bathing suit, shirts, shorts, tiny nail scissors, hairbrush, toothbrush, new one, all those things packed up. Yes, they were all there.

I dragged the pack outside, round back of the house,

all the way round, where hardly anyone went, except for Will, looking for sticks sometimes. Dropped to my hands and knees, I felt around, found that path, still there, worn down from all the times I'd dug down there, just me, never Will, he was too scared of dogs, was afraid a dog would be hiding down under there. I found the door, pushed it open.

I crawled down in, dragging my knapsack behind, felt with my hands for that smooth place, found it, that place where I always used to sit, found the long flat rock I had put there for a table, still there. My place. Mine. Still mine. Leaned against the wall, could still sit up, straight up, still wasn't too big to sit up, my head not even bumping against the rough ceiling above me.

I waited, let my eyes get used to the dark, but still light, plenty of light with the light of the moon shining between those slats that ran all the way round that crawl space.

And then, I began pulling stuff out of the knapsack, shirts, hairbrush, bathing suit, the nail scissors, held the nail scissors.

I started with the bathing suit, breathing harder now.

Straps on top — yes! — snipped, snipped them off, right off. Easy to do. Front. Then back. One side. Then the other.

Held those straps in my hands.

Then I started down the sides, cut a little piece here, more pieces there, it was easy to do, easy.

Snip, snip, snip, little bitty pieces fell all around me.

I heard other sounds then, wolflike sounds. Lord, who'd make a sound like that besides a wolf? Maybe a dog howling?

And then I heard another sound, padding, footstep sound? I stopped snipping, listened. A dog? Deer? No. Deer, they came on silent feet. Then what?

And still that howling sound that came from right nearby, right here, down in this space. Maybe there were ghosts and haunts, and maybe they were right here, under this porch, right by me?

And then the door opened, and Lord, there was a face, right up in my face, right there, crawling toward me. The face kept on coming, and there was a body, too, attached, and it was too big, too big for this space, but she kept on coming, coming.

"Go away!" I yelled, but she didn't stop.

And then Clara was in there, right inside my space, my space, where she shouldn't have come, and who asked her?

The howling got louder, moaning sounds, wolflike and I cried, "Don't!"

Still she came on, and then her big old arms came round me, and she was holding me tight, and I was fighting back, but she didn't let go, didn't let go, Lord, her arms were strong, and she didn't let go.

Didn't say anything, not a word, kept holding on, while I fought her like a wolf, was a wolf. Those sounds came out of my own throat, they did. But Clara was strong. She held me. She held me.

I stopped everything, stopped fighting, stopped everything. Too tired, too much. Even the howling and moaning stopped.

And then I felt it, felt it coming on. From inside, somewhere inside, it came up. Tears were on my face, down my cheeks, back into my ears.

I tried once more, just once, to get away, yelled, "Don't!"

But Clara just held me tighter, and then the crying came on. Lord, it came on, it did, it really did — it would never stop. I cried. Just like Will, I cried.

Chapter 20

Like wild things, we were like wild things. That's the first thing I thought when I next opened my eyes, blinking against the sun peeping in between the slats. We were like a bunch of wild pups, wolves or bears or foxes maybe, all three of us heaped together, asleep on the dirt floor there.

I was stretched out, Clara's lap my pillow, and right by my side was Will, one hand wrapped around his neck, the way he always sleeps, his other hand resting on my knee. But he wasn't sleeping now, was just looking at me, wide-eyed, and I looked up, around, and Clara, she was blinking at me, all three of us, looking at each other sleepy-like.

"What?" I said.

Clara just shrugged. "Guess we all started out here,

and I didn't see much sense in moving us, not once you were asleep. But I got to say, I'll be glad to get out of here."

I sat up, rubbed my face, rubbed my hands up and down my face. And then it all came back, sort of. I felt ashamed, shy, shouldn't have let her know, see those things.

I kept rubbing up my face, thinking how to be now, how to *be*.

"Gabby?" Will said, his voice all sleepy, baby sounding.

"What?" I said.

"Are you . . . are you okay now?"

"I'm okay," I said.

"Gabby?" Will said again. "Why were . . . ? I mean, you were crying!"

"So what?" I said, and I knew my voice was mean.

"Because of Daddy?" Will said.

I shot him a look.

"You scared me," Will said. "I was scared. You were screaming and carrying on, and I thought . . ."

"Tell you what, Will," Clara said. "Why don't we get on inside and I'll make you some peach pancakes."

"Goody!" Will answered, and he scrambled to his feet, and I just shook my head at him. Funny, he'd never eaten when Dad was gone, ate so little. But he'd been eating for Clara — all she had to do was ask him, tempt him with something, and he'd eat. So how come, how come for her, and not for me?

Didn't know, didn't matter.

All three of us crawled out of there then on hands and knees, came out blinking in the sunlight.

I straightened up, felt the cricks in my back, my knees — Lord, even my rear end hurt. And I was itchy, like sand fleas had gotten me, itchy, hot places on my ankles and feet.

We started on round to the front of the house, Clara leading, Will trailing by her side, stopping every little bit to pick up a twig or stick.

I held back, thinking, *Now what?* That's what I kept thinking: *Now what?*

He wasn't much, Dad wasn't, at least he wasn't the best, but he was something, wasn't he? He was something and he was ours! And he wasn't coming back anymore. And now what? Again I felt the tears, hot, flooding up, welling up, not from my eyes, but from somewhere else, deep inside, deep down, like from my chest, and I tried to swallow them down.

I looked around at the sun coming up, the dew shining on the grass, the big drops of wet bending each blade low, thought of going walking again — that helped, maybe walking through the woods. But I was tired, stiff, and Clara and Will, they were waiting for me up by the porch. Clara stood at the bottom of the steps, and up on the porch, Will had already sat down, cross-legged, was working on a twig thing.

I didn't want to talk, so when I went up to the steps, I ducked my head, headed past them.

But Clara, she stopped me. "Gabrielle," she said, and she used my whole name, the way Mom used to, the way Dad did when he was being specially nice, trying to make up after one of his binges or something.

I didn't answer, didn't look at her. But I waited for her words.

"Gabrielle," she said again.

I took a big breath, held it in, looked at her.

"You did what you had to," she said. "You had to. Mustn't be ashamed of what you have to do."

I ducked my head again — no need to remind me that I'd cried. Like a fool, I'd cried, like it would make anything better. And more, it was happening again. I could feel it happening, tears welling up in me all over again.

"Go ahead," Clara said. "Your daddy is dead and you should cry. You'll be better now."

Stupid, stupid thing to say. Before we had a dad, not much of a one, but we had one, here today, gone tomorrow, that kind of dad but at least we had one. No mom, but a dad. And now we had nothing. Couldn't even hope anymore.

I opened my mouth to tell her those things, but closed it up again.

"Listen to me," she said. She put a hand on my arm. "You listening?"

I looked at her. Of course I was listening. How could I not? She was right in my face.

"All right," she said when she saw she had my attention. "I'm not much of a mama, Lord knows I didn't do good enough with your daddy, and I don't know how I'll do with you two. But I'll do my best, and you two will, too. We'll manage somehow. Together, we will. Something else — we can do it right here, so you won't have to move."

I pulled back from her, frowned at her. What? Together we'll what? Live together? Who asked her? Who needed her?

"You go on home now," I said to her. I turned to Will then. "We'll be okay, just like always, right, Will? We'll be fine by ourselves."

But Will, he didn't answer, didn't even move. He had set down his twig thing and was sitting there, still, head bent, staring at the porch floor, so still, not even breathing, from the looks of it. He could have been one of those stone statues in the graveyard, those angels or doves or things that sit on the graves. And then he looked up at me, right at me, eyes wide like the wild deer that you come across in the meadow. And the look on his face was hopeful.

A dumb, hopeful look.

"Will?" I said.

He didn't answer, just kept looking back at me, holding still like that, real still. But I could hear him anyway, hear what he was saying silent-like, inside himself. *Please, Gabby,* he was saying, *please, please, please?*

I shook my head, breathed deep, turned away from him, looked out over the fields. I just kept looking out there, shaking my head, thinking.

Lord, how it had all changed. I'd known it from that very day when I first saw those people on the porch, saw Clara there, the county car. Knew it then, knew it now. Things were changed.

And now what? Now what?

"Gabby?" Will whispered. "If Clara stays, you can go to the ocean."

I started to say, I'm not going to the ocean. But instead, I just turned around, looked at them both, put out my hands . . .

It seemed then like everything grew still. Will was looking at me. Clara was looking at me. And they were both waiting. I shook my head, felt suddenly like the whole world was waiting, the whole world.

I turned away again, looked around me. The night breeze had blown itself away. The sun was up. The moon was up there, too, just a white shadow hanging in the sky, a child's moon, Mom used to call it when it showed itself in the day like that. The night creatures and deer had fled back to the woods. And here, on the porch . . .

I turned back to Will, Clara. Here on the porch, here was — what *was.* And this, too: It was all I had.

Dumb, I guess, to feel it so spelled out like that.

Dumb. Scary, too. But then, why not let it be, whatever would be?

But still, I'd been the mom, the dad, for a long time. No, no, not just the mom and dad — I'd been the everything for Will. For weeks at a time while Dad was gone, I was the everything for Will.

But Dad wasn't coming back to Will anymore. And he wasn't coming back to me anymore, either.

"You've been the mama for a long time," Clara said, like she was inside my head, thinking my thoughts along with me. "It doesn't mean you have to give it up all the way. Maybe just be the grown-up some of the time. Just maybe share it. You think you could?"

I still didn't answer, couldn't even think. Well, not true — I was thinking plenty, but nothing that made any sense.

"Gabby?" Will said.

I took a deep breath, then another, an easy one, and looked at Clara. "Maybe I will go to the ocean," I said.

And then I turned to Will, let my arms reach out to him, to hug him — it'd been a while.

He scrambled to his feet and came into my arms, and I hugged him up, hugged him good. It'd been a while. Such a while.

I've been to the ocean and I've been back, wrote so much when I was there, filled up two whole notebooks, and maybe someday — maybe someday I'll tell the whole story, the whole story, not just about the ocean, but the whole story of the life of Gabrielle Thackeray Blakely. Don't know why not. There's a story there to tell. Such a girl to tell about.

And oh, about the ocean: Mom was right about that ocean. And Clara, she was right, too. It's something else, it is. It roars and thunders and seems to scream at you, at least the winds and the seabirds do. And then it calms, and it whispers to you, like it's a mom who's telling you secrets, things to put you to sleep at night. And at night — Mom was right about this, too — the moon, it shines on the water, and it looks like two moons, it does, twin moons, just like Mom said.

Something else about the ocean: It works magic on you. We were just there three days, that's all, because all the rest of the time we were getting there, in the mountains, or on the road, even stopped in New York City, and Lord, is that something to see. I'll write about that, too, someday, in my own story of me. Anyway, those three days at the ocean were magic. When you just sit quiet, looking, listening to the wind and waves, things work out inside you like magic.

One thing I thought about a lot, even figured out, was

my voice. She wasn't just a voice, I figured. She was me. She was a part of me, that inside me, the one who knew what was what. She was harsh sometimes, mostly pointed out the bad things, but she was also smart. And maybe at times, I figured, maybe I have to fight with me, with my own self, just to sort things out some. There's been nobody else to sort them out with, not once Mom died. And so it's the way I do it, fight with myself, think it through, all sides of it. And sort it out. And I always do sort it out. I do.

Like this thing, this big important thing with Will. It happened right before we left. Will and I had gone walking across the fields in the moonlight, leaving Clara sitting on the porch, just looking up at the moon, rocking some. I needed to walk some but didn't want to be alone, and how's that for a shift in things? So Will and I, we went out just to the edge of the meadow in back, off by the woods, where we stood and watched deer come down from the woods, watched them drift into the meadow, quiet as shadows.

After watching awhile, Will slid his hand up into my hand, and he said, real quiet-like, "Gabby? Know what?"

"What?" I said.

Will took a deep, shaky breath, and then he said, "I've been making dogs!"

"*Dogs!*" I looked down at him. "Dogs? You mean, stick dogs?"

He nodded.

"You?" I said. "How come?"

He looked away, down at his feet. "Because," he said.

"But dogs?" I said. "You hate dogs!"

Will just shrugged. Then he took his hand out of mine, reached in his pocket, took something out, held it up. "Look," he said.

I put out my hand, and he laid something there, and even in the moonlight, I could see it was beautiful, a beautiful work of art, it was, a perfect, tiny dog.

It was just maybe four inches long, its head tilted to one side, its ears hanging low. There was even a tiny tongue hanging out of its mouth. And if you didn't know Will was scared to death of dogs, you'd think this was made by someone who loved dogs more than most anything, it was so sweet.

"Will!" I said, turning it this way and that. "Will, it's beautiful. It's . . . *real*."

"I know," Will said, and his voice was shy, the way it always gets when you say nice things about his work.

I held it out to him, and he took it back.

"But why, Will?" I said. "Why?"

He shrugged, but he looked up at me, that wide-eyed look, and I figured he knew why, just wasn't saying, maybe couldn't say?

And then suddenly, before either of us could say another word, there was this sound from a tree right near us, half scared me to death, an owl hooting. *Whoo, who,* it called, *whoo, who,* and Will, he suddenly threw back his head, and he called back, *whoo, who?*

I just looked at Will, laughed out loud. But that owl, he took it serious-like. I think he thought he was talking to another owl, because for a long time after, a long, long time, he kept on with Will. *Whoo, who,* he said. *Whoo, who?* Will called back. On and on they went, like a couple of old owl friends, catching up on news, or else maybe like new friends, introducing themselves one to the other.

I don't know how long we stopped there, Will being an owl, me just listening. Listening and thinking, thinking about that little stick dog. How come dogs? Dogs when he was scared to death of dogs. But then, looking at Will playing like that, his head thrown back, his lips bunching up to make another *Whoo, who* sound, I figured something, at least I thought I did. I could picture him, see him sitting on the porch, making a dog. He'd make it — a dog. He'd touch it, he'd mold it, he'd handle it — a dog! Maybe his hands were shaking when he did it — even fake things can be scary — but he did, he made a dog. And maybe another day, he'd make another dog, bigger, fiercer, and then another, cheat those fears, cheat them.

Yes. Cheat the fears, that's what you do, cheat them.

That was exactly what Mom meant, wasn't it?

Suddenly, above our heads, there was a whoosh of wings, and the woods got quiet again, and that owl, he'd gone off someplace, maybe to tell his family about that new owl that had taken up residence in the meadow.

Will tilted his head, listening, but when the owl didn't come back, didn't call anymore, Will turned to me. "I'll make an owl next," he said. "A baby owl and a mama owl." He took a big breath. "And maybe another dog," he said, real matter-of-fact-like.

A cloud scudded over the moon then, covering it an instant, and Will's hand crept up into mine, and we held each other tight.

Then together, Will and I turned back to home. I looked down at Will, felt his little hand soft and warm, content-like inside my own, and I thought about what Dad had said. Dad was right. Will was brave, he really was, the bravest boy of all.

And then I heard the voice, my voice, that inside one. She wasn't mocking me, nor fighting me, just being regular, just talking to me nicely, like maybe I was going to get along with myself awhile.

You're brave, too, she said, real soft-like. *You are really, really brave.*

I thought about that, found myself nodding, nodding.

Yes. Maybe so. Maybe so.